The Fourth Door

Mark Eugene Langner

Aliso Street Productions

To Victoria, for her sense

*   *   *   *
*

This is a work of fiction. Any similarity between characters and real persons, living or dead, is purely coincidental.

ISBN:
978-0-9840120-1-5

Printed in the U.S.A.

THE FOURTH DOOR
TABLE OF CONTENTS

PART ONE

PART TWO

PART THREE

PART FOUR

The Fourth Door

PART ONE

CHAPTER ONE
Good neighbors

Halla, a young Ministrant of Eator, welcomed a small and silly errand. It offered her a brief respite from the very source of her frustration. The High Minister's recent behavior was increasingly capricious. Now Elyda wanted, of all things, a jellycrisp.

The smooth stone wall of the Center opened at Halla's touch. She hastened along an inner path, her simple green gown shapeless about her. She pulled at it and tried to fluff her hair.

A side entrance admitted Halla to the bustling marketplace. Flags flapped overhead. High walls lined with vendors' booths slanted away from each other. The public areas of the city were all similar in shape, broad wedges that surrounded the Center. They, in turn, were encircled by the Great Path.

Beyond the Great Path lived the major population

* Chapter One *

of Eator, the Genexus. It seemed to Halla that most of them were there in the marketplace, it was so crowded. Dressed in bright colors, they milled about on their errands as vendors called to be included in their considerations. Everything would even out by the end of the day, but in the meantime there was sport to be had in the negotiation of a good deal.

Halla would visit Boz' booth. Boz, the baker, was dead but Aryla, his daughter, and her new husband, Rykos, had yet to change the name of the little establishment. Halla and Aryla were childhood friends.

There was something that Halla wanted to tell Aryla. Although Elyda, as High Minister, insisted that the recent attack on Yutor was an isolated incident, she had become increasingly agitated. Constantly the beleaguered city was whispered in her prayers. What, Halla wondered, provoked Elyda's supplications?

And now she wanted a jellycrisp. "Go immediately and get me one." Had Elyda so simply – and blithely – forgotten her anxiety? Or was it another indication of her growing infirmity? As Halla entered the marketplace she remembered that events had driven the previous High Minister to madness. Jovia had died on the same day as Boz.

Poor Aryla. Halla reminded herself that too easily

she forgot the trials of others. Boz, she knew, was keenly missed, especially now that Rykos, according to rumor, was commissioned by Elyda to work at home alone on a task of extreme importance. Aryla and her mother did their best to manage without them.

Booths below the high curve of the Center sold a variety of refreshments. The air was robust, sweet and savory. Tables under shady trees offered visitors relief from the rigors of the day. Halla was lucky. Only a short line waited at Boz' booth.

Although Aryla was plump and plain, a sweet expression made her pretty. Halla noted how tired she looked. "Can't you take a break?" she asked.

Overhearing her, Aryla's mother emerged from the back of the booth to wait on customers. After Halla selected Elyda's jellycrisp, she and Aryla found a nearby table where they could sit and visit.

Halla described how busy she was. Elyda was experiencing swings in behavior and depended upon her more and more. Had Halla been more perceptive she might have suspected that it wasn't Elyda who made use of her – or wanted again to taste a jellycrisp. Halla thought only of herself. She paused for a moment to let Aryla react to her news, but her friend seemed to have drifted off. "Aryla, are you listening to me?"

Something obviously preoccupied Aryla. She was acting like – Elyda. If Halla continued to describe the High Minister's recent behavior, she worried, would she sound critical of Aryla as well?

*

Aryla, indeed, wasn't listening to Halla – she herself was questioning her own mental state. There was something that she wanted to tell Halla, too, but she promised her father that she wouldn't.

By the recent moon Boz appeared to Aryla in a dream. There was less pepper and more salt to his hair. The glint in his eye was wiser. He explained Rykos' secret mission to Yutor.

"Rykos?" she cried. "Gone?"

Boz instructed his daughter not to let anyone, especially the family, know. "Tell them he's called to the Center. He'll return with a proposition. I urge you to consider it carefully. Let neither fear nor folly influence your decision." Aryla still heard his words.

It was Halla, however, who was speaking at the moment. She repeated her question. "Aryla, are you listening to me?"

Aryla could endure it no longer. "Halla, you won't believe what's happened. The other night, in a dream, my –"

Two hooded Monitors appeared, interrupting her. "You're needed in the Center," one of them advised.

"I'm coming," Halla sighed, explaining to Aryla, "Elyda wants her jellycrisp.

The other Monitor clarified, "We come for Aryla. You've wanted by the High Council."

"What?"

*

Six paths ran from the Center as if spokes of a wheel. Beyond the Great Path they bound the neighborhoods of the Genexus. Urban congestion gave way to gardens that stretched to the far fields. Around them grew the Wooden Wall, a defense of living trees. There the Genexus' world ended and, they were taught, a great forest began. It was home to the Woodswarder, men of legend and exaggeration who guarded the city.

The Genexus didn't know that the great forest was but a modest ring of trees that encircled Eator. Many such woods lay scattered about the vast grasslands of Kala. Had the Genexus known the true dimension of their protection, and of the evil that existed everywhere around it, the Ministration worried that they would live in constant fear.

Hours earlier there was consternation outside the Ring. Although it was known by Cyrll's captains that a party of Woodswarder, at Elyda's bidding, recently departed for Yutor, this morning a different party returned. Among them was Aryla's husband.

*

With her remaining powers of Kala, the powers by which she had transported herself and Rykos to Yutor, Ava attempted to transport herself, Rykos and Thayn back to Eator. The party fell short of its mark but, luckily, beyond the river. They avoided the island city of Tordawn and its Outcasts.

In his traveling robe Thayn looked like a Monitor, but he was every inch a Woodsward, tall and broad at the shoulder. He brushed the hair off his brow by habit and looked around them. Ava heard his thinking.

Incredulous, she asked aloud, "Rats?" Ava was a Ministrant. Friends since childhood, they later became stepsiblings and even better friends. Now, as valiant comrades, they returned from the liberation of Yutor.

"From the river." They heard one. "There."

Thayn pointed into the rippling grass and whispered quick words. A flash flew from his fingertip and smacked a rat squarely. It fell. In reply came a chorus of squeaks.

"Run."

"Hurry." Ava lost her wimple as they scrambled

away. Thayn stunned a few more rats and those that followed stopped to fight over the fallen.

A safe distance away, the friends stopped for a moment to catch their breath. "Oh, my." Ava let loose her long braid of red hair, recoiled it on top of her head and resecured it with a wooden pin.

"Ouch." Rykos always mimicked Ava when she adjusted her hair.

Rykos was a Genexus. He, too, had grown up with Ava and Thayn. As friends they were inseparable until, as the time of their Choosings grew near, Rykos' attentions turned to Aryla, the baker's daughter. Recently married, he was impatient to return to her now.

He looked around them. The grasslands seemed to stretch forever. "Couldn't you have gotten us a little closer?" he complained.

Ava considered an angry response but Thayn intervened, attributing their abbreviated passage to the wisdom of Kala. "Who would believe you were gone, Rykos, if they didn't witness your return? Besides, we aren't that far."

Ahead grew woods similar in appearance to countless others. They were hailed in advance by a scout. An interception party emerged from the Ring.

"Can you hear their thoughts?" Ava asked.

Thayn and Rykos nodded.

A Ministrant, Genexus and Woodsward – in the grasslands? Or were they Outcasts? Was it a trick of Vok? Confusion had quickly traveled from a nervous scout through his communicator to Tylos, their captain, and to Cyrll, the High Warden himself.

*

The Monitors escorted Aryla and Halla to the Center. Its seamless wall opened at their touch. They followed a broad hall that ran inside the circumference of the ancient stone edifice. Other hallways led them deep within the Center to the High Chamber.

Cyrll arrived wearing a robe that struggled to conceal his enormity. White hair belied a youthful face. He brought with him the interception party and those who came from Yutor.

At the dais stood the High Council. Among the older women was a new member, Yara. She filled the vacancy left by Jovia's passing and Elyda's appointment as High Minister. Her round face lit up at the sight of Ava.

Elyda, her face heavily wrinkled, whispered in silent prayer. Thayn, Ava and Rykos heard thoughts of nonsense as the High Warden reprimanded her aloud. "Did you not tell us, Elyda, that you sent Thayn to

Yutor after the others? He tells me a different story."

Elyda blinked, remembering events. Ava and Rykos had helped Thayn depart Eator through a passage
that she herself had sealed, the Third Door. In anger,
Elyda confined Ava and Rykos to their quarters and
charged them with meaningless tasks. Now they came
back from Yutor with Thayn. How was this possible?

It required a good deal of explanation. Aside from
Aryla nobody knew that Rykos, or for that matter, Ava,
had left Eator. Aryla related how Boz, her father, informed her in a dream.

Upon the passing of her predecessor, Elyda was
herself possessed by Vok. Her mind unraveled as the
others contributed their details to the tale. Poised to assist Vok in an assault on her own city, her mind wandered aimlessly after he fled through the Fourth Door.
She struggled to commensurate his lingering thoughts
with what the others now shared. Thayn and Ava described Yutor's destruction, liberation and renewal. In
conclusion, they requested recruits to resettle the city.

Elyda laughed and whispered to herself. She wandered from the room, her head jerking violently. Those
in the High Chamber heard a stifled scream. A passing
Ministrant found Elyda on the smooth stone floor of a
hallway arguing with an unseen force.

None among the senior Ministration dared to respond. Finally, Yara approached Ava. She promised, "We'll send to Yutor all that is required." Everyone stared at her, astonished at her audacity. By stepping forward, Yara became the acting High Minister.

*

"You want us to do what?" Aryla asked Rykos, unsure that she heard correctly. As Boz foretold, her new husband returned with a proposition.

"Yutor needs us," Rykos explained. "Aryla, you should see their children."

"Who's with them now?"

"Kaden, Owan and Jad."

"You left the children with *Woodswarder*?"

*

Thayn and Ava accompanied to Yutor a first party of volunteers, proud Ministration, Woodswarder and Genexus of Eator. Meanwhile a second party of volunteers was prepared. Among the first party were Rykos and Aryla's family. Brave and spirited, they intended to resettle Yutor. They would care for the city and its children. Owan and Jad returned to escort the second party. Powers of Kala continued to protect them.

It was earlier decided that, as its only surviving Woodsward, Kaden would serve as Yutor's High Warden. Ava would return as High Minister. She shielded her intention from Yara who expected Ava to remain in Eator as her consort. Instead, Ava found an irresistible sense of purpose attending to Yutor. It broke her heart to break Yara's heart, but this way they both had their own city to run.

With sincere appreciation Ava welcomed the new Ministration to Yutor. Ceremonies to purify and sanctify both the Center and the temple immediately commenced. Every building required their attention.

Kaden, as High Warden, wore no crown. His spirit had been broken into pieces by Vok and he was unpredictable in temperament. He greeted his recruits with a broad, sweeping gesture only to say, "Acquaint yourselves," and nothing more. He withdrew.

There were too few Woodswarder to offer Yutor but a pretense of protection, but prayers to Kala returned on the wind well-answered and settled about the city. Nobody unwelcome to Yutor would dare attempt to enter it.

Portions of every nexus had been readied and were waiting for new families to occupy them. Rykos in his capacity as Senior Peer and Aryla assisted the Genexus in the selection of suitable homes and distributed their charges among them. Although it was a cause for great joy, the children were witless, their faces vacant.

Thayn's time attending to the Genexus concluded as his services were no longer required. A visit to the Center found its residents at prayer.

The Ministration and the Genexus had lost them- selves – and found themselves – in their new activities. Thayn's place wasn't among them. His world waited beyond the Wooden Wall. He returned to the Ring.

A guard at the gate welcomed Thayn. Untouched by Vok's violence, this portion of the Ring arched high to a green canopy that was splattered with orange and red. The air was warm and fragrant.

The guard welcomed Thayn. "To what sector are you assigned?" he asked.

What sector? Thayn hadn't thought about it. He wanted to think of nothing. How inviting the Ring of Yutor was, its light and shadow chasing one another, breezes fluttering through the trees. Perhaps when Jad returned, they would settle here, too.

The guard added, "I would gladly serve you."

"What about your captain?"

"My captain would serve you too, I'm sure of it."

"What about Kaden?"

"We *know* you." At once the Ring of Yutor lost its warmth and color. Thayn realized that his plans were in jeopardy. He mustn't become a rival to Kaden, not even for a moment.

He left for Eator immediately.

*

How empty the grasslands felt. As Thayn neared Eator his powers, no longer needed, withdrew. Without them, he felt weak and his feet grew heavy.

Jad and Owan appeared in the distance. They led a second party of recruits to Yutor. Thayn walked wide around the Genexus, avoiding by habit needless contact with them. Instead, he reached out in thought to the Woodswarder. Would Jad still hear him?

Thayn and Jad met in a nearby stand of saplings. "We've only a moment."

Remembering his recent visit to the Diversionary, Thayn smiled and replied, "That's time enough."

*

Soft green enveloped Thayn as he entered the Ring of Eator. Leafy vaults opened overhead and shimmered in the wind. The air was moist and sweet.

Tylos dropped from a tree. He smiled. "Welcome, Woodsward. Don't think we were unaware of your arrival. Cyrll's waiting."

Thayn visited the wash station and emerged with fresh green bristlecloth at his side. He proceeded with

Tylos to the pavilion.

The captains stood, Tylos taking his place among them. Cyrll stood too, a massive man, his face enduringly young, his white hair tousled under a withered wreath. Thayn looked at Cyrll and beyond him. The trees, the faces, everything was so familiar.

He looked into the High Warden's eyes. Cyrll held a hand out to him. Conflicting emotions flooded over Thayn, sweeping away everything but the moment.

The pavilion blurred and went black.

*

Thayn looked up into the canopy. The world came back into focus. Cyrll knelt next to him, supporting him with a hand to his back. Softly Cyrll said, "I've dismissed the captains."

"What happened to me?"

"You're exhausted. It's to be expected as the powers of Kala take their leave of you. And you're home." Cyrll's words, his voice, comforted Thayn. Everything grew blurry again.

Cyrll picked Thayn up and carried him out of the pavilion. He sprang into the nearest sturdy tree, maneuvering with one arm and holding Thayn with the other. Working his way carefully, he climbed as high as he dared. A triple fork formed a secure place where

Thayn could rest.

Cyrll placed Thayn within its branches and retired. Thayn moaned softly. His eyes fluttered, green as the leaves around him. He slept for days.

Thayn dreamt of something sweet. Smoke and herbs. Shadows danced in a dark clearing. The great gray vault glowed above him. Thayn stepped among feathery ferns and into the light of a fire. He whirled around.

An arm met another and broke. *Crack.* A third arm shattered the second. *Crack.* A fourth arm sliced the air to meet the third. *Crack.* Others waited. Every arm was broken by the next. It didn't matter to whom they belonged, only that the breaking continued.

Perpetuity. The arms grew younger and younger. "No," Thayn cried in his dream.

"No," he echoed aloud. He scrambled to his feet, balancing himself on the smooth branch of a tall tree, drenched in sweat.

CHAPTER TWO
Good friends

The breaking of arms. That same dream. What, Thayn wondered, if it had come true? If the chain had continued? If Thayn hadn't broken it?

He considered likely answers to his questions. The tree in which he rested would be withered. The Ring that surrounded Eator would be broken and burnt. The Wooden Wall would lay splintered in the fields.

Thayn walked in thought throughout the city. The walls that bordered the outer paths would have fallen. The stones that built the congested dwellings of the Genexus would have collapsed. Thayn contemplated the ruins of the household of his own family. It had always resounded with life.

He imagined wanton devastation. A leaf that flew through the air distracted Thayn and freed him from his thoughts. More leaves fell as a breeze found the Ring.

The ceiling fluttered.

Still standing in a sweat, Thayn secured his bristle-cloth at his side. He didn't want to dream anymore. He didn't want to think. Thinking and dreams made his head hurt.

He wanted to move about the Ring, but not along the bridging or pathways used by the other Woods-warder. Thayn didn't want to answer to them. He pulled himself through the higher branches.

Thayn reached the Wooden Wall. He could see the fields of Eator. Some sections were in harvest while others were recently planted. Beyond the fields the dwellings of the Genexus stood tall and intact. Within them the public buildings encircled the pristine Center. Afternoon sunlight glanced off its high curved wall.

All was as it should be. It seemed impossible. So much had happened, but so little had changed. Thayn reminded himself that, as a Woodsward, this was his goal.

Perhaps there was greater awareness in Eator of the world beyond the Wooden Wall, but it would fade. The families recruited to resettle Yutor were small and complete within themselves. Their absence would be either overlooked or excused. The Genexus didn't eas-ily think beyond the particulars of daily life.

* Chapter Two *

Thayn saw men working in the fields, splotches of color, and heard children playing. He smiled. Soon the Genexus would return home. They would prepare their evening meals and share news of the day. Children would study. Families would dye and spin bristle and weave their cloth. Then they would put the day to rest. This is what Thayn protected.

From the Center, carried on a gentle breeze, Thayn could hear a ringing of bells. He had keen ears. *Bong. Bong. Ding.* A High Council was beginning. Yara, the acting High Minister, and her elder subordinates would attend to the affairs of the city.

Below him Thayn heard Woodswarder. Some hurried on errands. Others visited in the clearings. Yes, everything was right.

Thayn was weary. As if houseguests who, called home abruptly, leave their quarters in disarray, so the powers of Kala had left Thayn. He missed them. His body ached and his mind wandered.

He returned through the trees. *"Trea baab caac daad."* What if those words hadn't been spoken? New thoughts came to him. Without interference, the Third Door would have opened. Vok easily would have escaped through it and Thayn would have pursued him. How different would his world be?

Thayn imagined how he would track Vok. It was up to him, he felt, to undo his uncle's evil. He owed it to his father and Arlos, Jovia and Elyda, and to the people of Yutor whom Vok had destroyed. He would hunt Vok wherever he attempted to hide, every crevice, every crag. They would each sense the other, the first always just ahead of the second, and to either of them rest would never come. This Thayn imagined.

He returned to his high branch and settled again into its fork. Thayn lapsed into a troubled slumber.

*

Moonlight slipped through the leaves. The glow of the Ring was faint in the canopy. It wasn't yet morning.

Leaves rattled. It was windy again, rocking the fork against which Thayn rested. It lowered suddenly. Thayn reached out to steady himself. The limb that he grasped was warm.

Thayn looked up. "Cyrll?"

"You've got me there," Cyrll laughed.

Thayn greeted the High Warden and stood.

"You're better," Cyrll noted. "Stronger."

"I feel better, yes."

"The Ring has waited to honor you. I've respected your need for rest. But will you come with me?"

"Of course. Where?" Thayn asked.

"To the pavilion. There's but one soul there who waits to see you."

"Who – ?" Cyrll stepped off the branch, descending. The fork in which Thayn slept rose in the air.

"Travel from up there if you wish," Cyrll called to him. "The higher branches won't support me."

Thayn waited for a few minutes, wanting to make sure that his head was clear before setting out in the faint glow of night. He rubbed his brow and stretched a little to limber up.

He started off for the pavilion, intending to visit a wash station along the way. Gusty breezes pulled at the branches. Thayn moved through them slowly but surely, careful to secure every footing and hold.

He descended to the floor of the Ring. A group of Woodswarder passed him on the path, one of them younger than the others. White bristlecloth hung at his side. The younger Woodsward exclaimed excitedly, "Look, it's Thayn."

An elder Woodsward, his mentor, hurried after him. "Yes." He glanced at Thayn apologetically, as if to acknowledge that everybody but his foolish charge knew that Thayn wished to be undisturbed.

Thayn smiled at him. The newcomer was on his

First Task. Thayn recognized him from school.

"May I greet you?" the young Woodsward asked.

"Now, come," his mentor replied, pulling him.

"It's all right," Thayn told him. "Yes, of course."

The young Woodsward fell to one knee.

Greeted, Thayn continued a short way to the wash station. He quickly emerged, refreshed, and made his way to the High Camp. Thayn entered the gnarlwood pavilion.

Cyrll sat behind a fallen log. Across from him, his back to Thayn, sat an elder. The two men spoke softly in quick conversation. "I didn't know of it," Cyrll exclaimed.

"We learn even in death," squeaked the old man.

Thayn brightened. "Lor? Is that really you? Are you back – alive?" He hurried to greet his own old mentor. Lor died the same night as Boz and Jovia.

Lor turned. "Stop." His voice was shrill.

Cyrll laughed.

"Stay away." Lor held up a hand. "Don't rush me. I'm not strong."

Thayn stopped.

"No, I'm not alive. But I'm more than a thought. As such, yes, I'm back, but just for a moment. And, for the moment, if you like, we may say I am real."

Lor smiled. "So, come, but gently, with fitting manner and decorum – "

Thayn quickly knelt.

" – not like some clumsy – oh."

Thayn kissed him.

"No better than you," Lor complained to Cyrll.

Cyrll laughed again.

"But you have done well," Lor acknowledged. As he greeted Thayn he grew increasingly insubstantial. Cyrll helped Lor to his feet and Thayn could see the High Warden's palm against the old man's back.

"Don't exert yourself," Cyrll warned him.

"It's time to go." Lor turned to Thayn. "I told you to tell me everything you knew of Kala and I would tell you more. Instead, from you we have learned even more than that.

"We died, we're dead, yes, but we haven't gone far. As stewards of the temple of Kala we've lingered to help you, to support you, and, as I've said, you have done well. Events, however, have progressed beyond our present level of understanding.

"He's gone," Lor continued, meaning Vok. "We didn't think beyond the land. No.

"A new time has commenced with the young Ministrant's response." He meant Ava. "We didn't know it would happen.

"But it has." Lor repeated, "And he's gone. Don't you feel your powers decline? It's over."

"Over?" Thayn remembered his dream and asked, "What about those Vok took with him?"

Lor and Cyrll exchanged an uncomfortable glance. "Unfortunate," Lor admitted.

"Unfortunate – ? But aren't they, as heirs of Kala, entitled to – ?"

" – to what? Don't think of it. They're beyond our reach."

"What about the Fourth Door?"

"I'm telling you, we don't know. We know more than we did, but there's even more we don't. There's nothing you can do." Lor grew increasingly impatient. "We're old. We're dead. It's over."

"Over?" Thayn repeated.

"It's time for us to join the incorporeal." Cyrll pulled Thayn away.

The ground shook. Lor stood in the center of the pavilion. High above a violent rustle disturbed the canopy.

Through it came the hand of Kala. Earthy fingers wrapped Lor in a firm grasp and retreated, showering the pavilion with sand.

* Chapter Two *

*

Lor was returned to the temple of Kala. Before him opened a cavern of white crystal. Its walls pooled and glinted with light.

"Come, Lor," Jovia called.

*

The ground under Thayn and Cyrll grew calm and the canopy sprang back into place. Thayn stared at the spot where Lor had stood. "I miss him already."

Cyrll closed his eyes and his expression narrowed. He was in communication with someone. After a moment his face relaxed and his eyes opened again. Cyrll smiled. "Owan and Jad – they're back from Yutor."

"Jad?" Thayn took a step toward the doorway before stopping himself. He reminded himself that he served at the pleasure of the High Warden.

"They're leaving Tylos' tower. Go."

Thayn ran from the pavilion, taking the main paths, moving too quickly to be delayed by others. He could hear Jad ahead, singing.

CHAPTER FOUR
Partings

Thayn had shared powers of Kala with Owan and Jad during the liberation of Yutor. Outcasts fled at the sight of them. Their powers protected the resettlement parties. On their way back, Owan and Jad's powers waned prematurely. Owan complained, "I'm so tired."

"We're not home yet."

Outcasts fought for control of Tordawn. To avoid capture the Woodswarder relied on their wiles, convincing rivals that they were traitors from the other side. They crossed the island in several stages and hid in bramble along the shore until dark. Using the guide rope, hand over hand, they forded the river.

The bank was thick with rats. "Run."

Owan and Jad continued to Eator by moonlight. A scout sensed them and, with an interception party, they reported to Tylos' tower. Tylos, on behalf of the High

Warden, promised the Woodswarder a great reception in their honor. First, Owan and Jad needed to sleep. They headed for the bower that they had previously shared with Kaden. Thayn found them on the path.

"Thayn," Jad exclaimed.

"You're back." Thayn ran to them.

"Our powers," Owan complained, "they're gone."

"They're no longer needed."

"I wish they would have lasted a little longer. We barely made it past the island." Owan examined a rat bite. "We've been running for *hours*."

"We're home now. We'll tend to our needs," Jad replied patiently. He asked Thayn, "How are you?"

"Better."

Owan started along the path again.

"We haven't slept," Jad explained as they followed Owan. "Do you want to join us?"

"Not if you really need to sleep."

Jad smiled. "There's going to be a reception, Ty-los says."

"After that, then."

"It's in your honor, too."

"I haven't much been in the mood for company. Not lately. Only tonight, to see Lor."

"Lor, really?" Jad yawned. He was interested, but

exhausted. He tried his best not to yawn again, but he couldn't help it. "I'm sorry."

Thayn replied, mocking Owan, "I understand. After all, you've been running for *hours*."

"It's because the powers you shared with us are gone, isn't it?"

"Yes."

"I can only imagine how *you* feel."

It was more than that – Jad *knew*. With his words and reassuring smile, everything was as it should be. As once with Arlos, answers came to Thayn in response to unasked questions. Worries melted away and the air seemed to embrace him. It was more than Jad's words – or less than them – it didn't matter. Jad needn't say anything, only stand there and be Jad.

They followed Owan along a path through the understory to the nearest wash station. Thayn sat against the trunk of a tree and waited until Jad emerged, refreshed. "Now I really need to sleep." He brushed the hair off Thayn's brow.

Thayn stood. "I'll come when you wake up."

Kissing him, Jad asked, "How will you know?"

"Some powers are still my own."

*

Thayn climbed through the canopy. The branches

seemed springy beneath him. He returned to the tree where he kept himself lately and found the fork in which he lay.

The day was poised to begin, still but expectant. Thayn stretched. He thought about everything that had happened lately. Perhaps he'd attend the reception after all. It was inevitable that he return to the company of others. They would honor him later if not sooner. With Jad at his side, he'd consider it.

With Jad at his side, Thayn mused, he'd consider anything. So deciding, he fell into his first restful sleep since his return to Eator. It lasted most of the day.

*

Thayn slept until a drop of rain landed squarely on his forehead. He climbed down out of the trees. Food carts rattled by. A pair of Woodswarder returned them, nearly empty, to the sector gate. As Thayn selected the last remaining sweetloaf he overheard their conversation and learned of Elyda's passing.

With the news came a rumor that she died by her own hand. Thayn stared after the cart as it continued on its way. The idea frightened him. Why would Elyda want to kill herself? Did Vok continue to control her from his distant situation out in the desert? Could his thinking reach so far? Or was her death in response to a remnant of Vok's thought to which Elyda held too tightly?

Thayn sensed Jad awake. He wrapped the sweet-loaf in his bristlecloth to protect it from the rain and hurried to their bower. Owan still slept. Jad welcomed Thayn but, by his expression could tell that something was wrong. Thayn shared the news of Elyda.

Jad said nothing, but Thayn knew that Jad, too, thought of Vok. They sat for a moment in silence until Owan awoke. He stretched, groaning sleepily, "Food? Good, I'm starved," and reached for the sweetloaf.

Jad looked at him crossly.

"What?"

"It's Elyda. She's dead."

"Dead? When? Just now?"

"Yes."

"How terrible. So it's raining, too."

"Yes. There'll be a Rotation tonight."

The Ministration had prepared Elyda for her rest in the Fallow Field. Already the Genexus paid their last respects. Monitors selected wood for her pyre. There would be no other activities in Eator today or tomor-row.

At dusk the Woodswarder would begin through the Ring at a measured pace in the same direction. They would enter the Fallow Field and walk along the inner curve of the Wooden Wall. As they passed their own small shrine, prayers would be offered for Elyda's gentle passing. The Woodswarder would continue walking until they stood where they started, at no point leaving any portion of the city undefended.

"And no reception for us," Owan complained, rolling over and burrowing back into the mulch. "Call me when it's time to go."

Thayn looked from Jad to Owan and back again. How different they were. Owan was a faithful comrade and true friend. He and Thayn had grown close, but only up to a point.

Jad, on the other hand, seemed to Thayn to be an extension of his own soul. Even without the powers of Kala, they seemed to know each other's thinking and, in whispers, shared their thoughts. "Poor Elyda."

Jad suggested, "Her passing is for the best. Kala has called her. I'm sorry about the reception, though."

"I'm not."

"You deserve it, Thayn. You've restored a great city."

"We all did."

"Wouldn't you have come to the reception," Jad asked, "really?"

"I don't know."

"Why not?"

Thayn shook his head and sighed. "They wouldn't know what they're honoring."

"What do you mean?"

"They don't understand."

"Understand what – ? I won't either, Thayn, if you don't tell me."

Thayn shrugged. "Vok."

"I was afraid that's what you meant."

"See?"

"It doesn't make any difference." Jad attempted to comfort Thayn, but he pulled away. "You're not responsible for what your uncle's done."

"So I shouldn't be honored for trying to – undo – it, either. Not that I ever could."

"You're no less a victim than anyone."

"I don't want to be a victim." Unexpectedly, he buried himself in Jad's embrace.

*

Dusk enveloped Eator. A call echoed and the Rotation of the Ring began. "Owan, it's time to go."

The rain continued. Thayn and Jad walked side by side, slowly and patiently. The Woodswarder kept their groups small and evenly spaced. Owan went ahead of them, sullen, obviously thinking about the missed reception. Several of his friends dropped from the trees. Thayn could hear Owan tell them of his adventures.

They passed through the Wooden Wall and in a single file along the edge of the Fallow Field. Its herbs and grasses, fragrant, were heavy with rain. Pausing at their simple shrine, Thayn looked across at the temple of Eator. He felt a surge of inexplicable loneliness.

The Rotation, in time, was complete. As they arrived outside the bower, the rain stopped.

"I'll be back later," Owan told Jad and Thayn. He went with the others. They would visit a few of his favorite clearings and Owan's friends, at least, would welcome him home.

*

"Tell me about Lor," Jad requested, attempting to stifle the first yawn in another round of them. They lay on the soft mulch of the bower floor.

Thayn told Jad about their meeting in the pavilion. He related how Boz, Jovia and Lor lingered in support of Yutor. Now that Vok was gone, they joined the incorporeal. "Everything's back the way it was. Except for – " Thayn shrugged.

"Except for what?"

"Except for those Vok took with him." Thayn referred to the stolen youth of Kala. "Except for them."

"They're gone."

"Something must be done."

"There's nothing you can do." Jad repeated Lor's words.

"They're beyond my reach?"

With a final yawn Jad surrendered to sleep, mumbling, "Sorry, I'm so – "

Thayn sat in silence until he dozed off, too – and he dreamt. As usual, an arm swept out. *Crack.* Then a second arm. *Crack.* A third arm. Thayn couldn't stop their breaking. "No," he cried. He awoke with a start, again buried in Jad's embrace.

*

"It's just not right," Owan declared, returning unexpectedly to the bower. Thayn and Jad roused to become, for a last time, his drowsy company.

"What's not right?" Jad asked Owan.

"Nothing's right. Nobody knows what really happened. Nobody knows what's going on."

Thayn sat up. He looked at Owan. "I think I know what you mean. Tell me more."

"We went to one of my favorite clearings. I told everybody about our mission. They said, 'Oh, yes' and

'I see' – but they *don't* know and they *can't* see. They don't know what it was like. Not the way we do."

"They can't help it," Jad explained.

"It doesn't matter."

"It'll be different," Jad suggested, "after the reception."

Owan made a disrespectful gesture. "To this with the reception."

Jad exclaimed, "Owan – "

"They've no idea," Owan continued. "They don't know what they honor."

"Yes," Thayn agreed. He looked at Jad. "See?"

Jad considered for a moment and shook his head. "It's not the same."

"I've spoken with Cyrll," Owan announced. "I'm going back to Yutor."

"What?"

"I want to be with Kaden."

Thayn and Jad glanced at each other, both surprised and smiling. "Of course."

*

Owan left the next morning. He was resolute to return to Yutor and Kaden. Although he possessed no powers but his own, he stood formidable. Thayn and Jad pitied any Outcast who stood or rat that squeaked in his way.

*

Jad recovered quickly from the passing of Kala's powers and assumed a standard rotation of duties. Thayn continued to experience a protracted convalescence. He felt, whenever Jad was away, the loneliness that he experienced at Elyda's funeral. He puzzled out the reason. Jovia, Lor, Boz and now Elyda had passed away. Ava, Rykos and now Owan were in Yutor with Kaden. Among those who shared in Thayn's adventures only Jad remained.

So much had happened, and all of it of such importance, and Thayn sat by himself among the ferns wondering, to what purpose was it?

Cyrll interrupted his solitude to offer Thayn a great honor, a captain's apprenticeship. Traditionally such training was reserved for older Woodswarder. "The only other candidate near your age who comes to mind was a young Woodsward named Lor."

Thayn was astonished both at Cyrll's offer and at the idea of Lor ever once having been a young man like him. "Sometimes I realize how little I really know about him."

"He was the youngest Woodsward to serve as High Warden, too," Cyrll added. Thayn remembered from

his lessons that two High Wardens served terms be-
tween Lor and Cyrll. Both of them had died before
Thayn's Choosing. "Lor lived long into his retirement.
He was waiting."

"For what?"

"For *whom*. You."

"I wasn't that important to him." Thayn shook his
head. "And he's gone."

"You allowed him to leave."

"I don't understand."

"I didn't think so. Nor do you realize that Lor has
bequeathed to you a great responsibility."

"What responsibility?" Thayn asked.

"A responsibility that begins with captains' training."

Thayn smiled at the High Warden's persistence.
He tried his best to describe his reluctance. "Others –
they don't understand – "

"Owan has made that clear to me, yes. He'll serve
Kaden well."

"Yes."

"Whom do you serve, Thayn?"

"I serve you."

"You serve no one less than Kala himself. Your
weakness as his powers take leave of you is a measure

of your strength, a measure of the trust he places in you.

"As for 'others', they understand the experiences they share with you. I know of your adventures only through communion with Lor, and only I know. You have yet to attend a reception. Sitting here by yourself, Thayn, you and the others share *nothing*. Don't you see?

"Captains' training will be challenging, perhaps, but Jad will support you," the High Warden concluded. "I know Jad's mind. Another measure of your character is his absolute faith in you. In Jad's eyes you will never fail."

CHAPTER FOUR
The Fourth Door

"A captain's apprenticeship?" Jad asked. His next question was unexpectedly difficult for Thayn to answer. "Do you want to be a captain?"

Thayn thought for a moment. "I don't think so. I just want to be like everybody else."

"It's too late for that," Jad laughed. "You probably already know more than all of Cyrll's captains put together. No wonder he's recruiting you. You might as well accept."

Thayn and Jad found an empty hollow near the High Camp. Around several saplings they wove vine to build a snug bower for themselves.

Captains' training for Thayn was much as school had been. He read books and shared reflections with other Woodswarder. He had previously scanned many of the books as an agent of Vok. He was surprised at how much he remembered – unaware of the knowledge that he possessed.

Some information about the Ring, however, was new to Thayn. Either these books weren't available in the Forbidden Room or Vok hadn't sought them.

One book explained how the political structure of the Ring formalized what came naturally. The Woodswarder served in concentrated shifts. Otherwise they were free to roam the Ring. The lack of structure was by design. Almost all Woodswarder came and went as equals, entertaining themselves and, at the same time, protecting the city as a matter of course.

Prescribed pastimes included acrobatics and aerial work. Countless hours were spent practicing and performing. Such activity embodied the ways of Kala, purpose, utility and beauty. It maintained among its participants a quality of life to which they easily devoted themselves.

*

Jad was due back from duty. Presently he tended the berry patches. Thayn sat waiting in their bower after captains' training. Something had caught his eye.

A vine grew through their bower wall and, upon it, a bud had formed. Thayn hadn't noticed it until, as the sun set, the bud swelled. As it opened, a petal caught on a tendril. The bud continued to open, contorted, until with a release of pent up energy the blossom sprang up and down, pale and deeply throated. It reminded Thayn of idleflower. So simple and complex. Thayn never felt a greater sense of peace.

*

That night a bright moon traveled above the leafy canopy. "Thayn?" He opened his eyes and sat up. Thayn almost recognized the voice. He heard it again.

"Come to me," it called. Thayn tilted his head to listen better. Where was the voice coming from – outside or inside his head? To whom did it belong?

Yara?

*

Jovia, then Elyda, and now Yara served as High Minister of Eator. Thayn hadn't liked her as a teacher at school. She was always horning in on his and Ava's business. He didn't much like her now.

"Jad will sleep until you return. Come."

Thayn left Jad snoring in the spongy mulch and slipped through an open gate into the city, obtaining a robe along the way. He met Yara in the back of the library. Her round face had grown thinner with care.

There was an awkward silence. Thayn knew that he should say something pleasant to her as High Minister, but he worried that he wouldn't sound sincere.

Instead, Yara explained, "I've not called you for an audience since your return from Yutor as I understood you requested solitude. You know, of course, in what esteem we all hold you – and Ava."

"And Rykos," Thayn reminded her.

"Yes."

"And the others who – "

Yara interrupted. "Thayn, I need your help. You want to help, don't you?"

Did it go without saying?

"I'm sensing something and I don't know how to respond to it," she continued.

Thayn scrutinized Yara. Her resolute expression was unflattering. Squinting eyes balanced atop flushing round cheeks. Thayn detected in her no ill intention – Yara didn't attempt to annoy him – but her lack of awareness bothered him all the more. Yara had her own agenda and saw everything in relation to it. It was irritating, Thayn thought, but perhaps a good quality in a High Minister.

"What do you sense?" he asked.

"Thoughts reaching past me out into the city."

"Whose thoughts?"

"And tidings from throughout the land."

41

"Tidings?" Thayn wasn't exactly sure what she meant. "What – ?"

"I can't tell – don't think I haven't tried." Yara was clearly frustrated. Thayn almost felt sorry for her. "I've only one option remaining."

"What's that?"

"To ask for your help."

"I don't have any power to – "

"I do. A little piece." She held a fingertip to the side of her head. "Jovia willed it to Elyda and now it's mine. But I need your cooperation."

"What do you want to do?"

"I want to give it to you. Here." With her other hand, Yara pointed a finger at Thayn.

He pulled away. "What? Why? What will I do with it?"

"You'll figure it out. You'll know."

Thayn hesitated. He was suspicious of power that came from Elyda, but if its source was Jovia, perhaps that was different. Taking a deep breath, he let Yara touch his temple. He brought his own fingers to the other side of his head as it filled with familiar sensations. "Don't move." Yara and Thayn stood side by side, her fingertip connecting them.

The power was faint, coming as a memory from

Jovia to Elyda and through Yara to him, but undeniable. He perceived voices, several voices all talking at the same time. He perceived ears straining to hear, but none of them heard a word.

It was High Ministers from throughout the land. Previously by Jovia's powers they had been convened. Now that she had passed, none among them was able to call them together. Their current attempt at a summit was failing.

Thayn concentrated. Several High Ministers flickered into substance before them. Yara stepped away from Thayn, extending a hand to greet them. They disappeared.

"Don't move," Thayn scolded her, "if you really want to do this. Jovia's memory is weak. You have to help me support it."

"I need to welcome them. It's protocol."

"If we can bring them here at all, we're doing well enough. You can practice your hospitality later – now *think*." Yara resumed her position and again they concentrated. The High Ministers reappeared.

Ava arrived. She immediately sensed the fragility of Jovia's power. "Yara, don't falter in your attention or we'll all be gone. I'll greet our guests.

"My fellow High Ministers," Ava addressed the

others in thought, "both Yara and I, new to your company, are humble before you. Yara focuses her efforts on keeping our summit intact as assisted by Thayn, Woodsward of Eator. Our time together is precious. Quickly, share your news."

They spoke without words. "Our Chosen – "

"Several of our Chosen – "

" – have disappeared."

"What?" Thayn exclaimed, his concentration wavering. In response, the High Ministers flickered.

"No," Ava cried aloud. Thayn returned to task and she urged the High Ministers, "Continue."

"Their parents are at a loss."

"At wit's end."

"How many are missing?"

"Six."

"Seven."

Most of the numbers, so far, were about the same.

"We continue to search for them."

"Are there any signs of violence?"

"No."

"Intrusion?"

"None."

The High Ministers shook their heads. There was little else to share.

"Shall we conclude, then?" Ava asked. "Perhaps enough power will linger for us to meet again. Thank you, all."

One by one the High Ministers disappeared.

"Yara – Thayn – try to hold me here a moment." Ava remained, pouting. Her image was faint. She asked Thayn, "What do you think?"

"Vok," Thayn replied.

"How?"

"I don't know – yet." Ava and Yara both looked at him. "I'll have to figure it out."

Ava reached out to touch Thayn's shoulder. Yara took advantage of the opportunity, almost kissing her, but Thayn pulled away in response to her proximity. "Oh," Yara exclaimed angrily as Ava disappeared.

Thayn didn't notice. Both he and Yara lost themselves in their respective thoughts. Finally Thayn decided aloud, "I'll begin tomorrow."

*

While Thayn met with Yara, Jad slept fitfully. He was visited by a dream that was not his own, but one that he recognized from Thayn's telling of it. An arm swept out of the shadows. Jad attempted to deflect it. It broke. *Crack*. A third arm shattered his own. *Crack*. A fourth arm sliced the air to meet the third.

Crack. Others waited.

Where was Thayn? Every arm was younger than the last. "No," Jad cried. He awoke, alone, and paced until Thayn returned.

"Yara told me you'd sleep until I got back," Thayn apologized.

"I had a bad dream." Jad described it and Thayn's eyes grew wide. In turn, he told Jad about the summit of High Ministers and his decision to search for the stolen youth of Kala.

"Where will you go?" Jad asked.

Thayn admitted, "I don't know."

*

The mulch never felt softer. Thayn looked up at a sky that pulsed with stars and he fell asleep, but only for a moment. The pulsation produced a painful sensation. He rubbed his head.

Something was wrong. What was it?

There were no stars beneath the canopy. The sensation continued, but it didn't come from the sky or Thayn's dreams. It came from the city. "What?"

In response to another pulsation Thayn felt great powers return to him, more intense and complete than ever. Jad awoke and Thayn shared them with him.

"Oh."

Yet another pulsation. Jad spontaneously winced and ducked his shoulders.

"Let's go," he and Thayn agreed simultaneously. They hurried to the Wooden Wall, making their own path through the trees. Woodswarder whom they encountered dodged out of the way.

Thayn pulled two robes out of a wash station. On previous visits to the city he had found the sector gates open or their guards asleep. This time Jad called to the guards to open the gate and, pending communication with Cyrll, they refused.

"No time. Follow me," Thayn cried. He and Jad scaled the Wooden Wall, a feat made possible only by the returning powers of Kala. They scrambled down the other side and dropped into the far fields.

Hopping a wall, they ran along an outer path. The pulsation continued. Like so many shooting stars the pulses originated from the Center and burst overhead, falling into the neighborhoods of the Genexus.

Thayn and Jad bound up several steps to the Center and banged on its smooth stone wall. There was no response. They ran back to the Great Path and, hearing footsteps, hid in the shadow of a doorway. A young man and his parents, all dressed in green, walked past without a word. They carried small stone jars.

Another pulse flew overhead. Reluctant to abandon the family, but unwilling to split up, Thayn and Jad decided to follow the pulse to its landing place. They defied custom by entering a nexus. "That way," Jad pointed.

They followed a narrow walkway that made its way among the congested dwellings of the Genexus. Passing an open doorway Thayn noticed a yellow spill on the stoop. He touched a fingertip to it and tasted it. "Honeydrop?"

They entered a tidy household. Colorful weavings decorated a handsome room. Two Genexus, a husband and wife, stared at Thayn and Jad, speechless. Thayn reached out to them in thought. With a grimace they returned to the moment.

"Monitors – but – ?" the woman cried.

"Why are you here?" the man demanded.

"Your son – ?" Jad asked.

"Or daughter – ?" Thayn inquired.

"She's asleep. In bed, as we all should be."

"You've been asleep dressed in your best green tunic and gown?"

The husband and wife looked at each other, bewildered. Other members of the household came from their rooms. One asked, "Where's Tallia?"

"What?"

"She's not in her room."

Tallia's mother ran down the hall. She returned moments later, breathless and sobbing.

"Who made the honeydrop?" Thayn asked, looking at Tallia's father. "You?"

"No, I – " Both he and Tallia's mother shook their heads in denial, although her gown and his tunic were splattered with yellow.

Thayn quickly communicated to Jad in thought, "Their memory has been erased, and will require cleansing of our visit, too, I'm afraid. Jad, shield your mind against me."

Jad blocked Thayn from his thinking.

"I've never tried this – I hope it works." Thayn whispered quick words. Tallia's family slowly relaxed and, without another word, retreated to their rooms.

*

"The family we passed earlier, and these parents, why are they dressed up?" Jad asked.

"What a dut I've been," Thayn realized.

"Both of us."

"Let me find Yara." Thayn concentrated. After a moment he reported, "She's in her room, but she must not sense me."

They returned to the Great Path. "Let's hurry."

Jad followed Thayn into the library. They gained access to the Center by a way that Thayn was surprised to remember, through a reading room in the rear. The wall opened at the touch of his palm. They entered the hall that ran inside the circumference of the Center.

"Try Yara again," Jad suggested. Thayn thought that she sensed him this time, but he couldn't be sure.

The pulsation recommenced. Thayn and Jad continued along several corridors. As they neared the Hall of Choosing they overtook the same son and parents from whom they hid in the Great Path. "It's his time." The proud parents smiled dotingly at their dazed son. All three of them carried jars of honeydrop.

Thayn reached into their thoughts but their minds withdrew from him. They flinched in response to his probing until honeydrop splashed everywhere. Much too quickly their faces relaxed.

They stared into space with the same lack of expression that Thayn's father wore. Thayn looked at them in horror. "No." Their minds were closed.

"Come," Jad urged him.

"I didn't do this," Thayn protested.

Jad pulled him along the corridor. The stone under them shook. "What's that?"

Thayn recognized the sound. "Hurry." Jad scrambled after him. They entered the Hall of Choosing to find the Fourth Door open.

Another young man stood in it. He held several jars of honeydrop, too. Thayn hesitated, but he was already too late. The Fourth Door snapped shut between them.

Jad stared at the young man's parents, incredulous. They smiled complacently in return. "Don't you know what's happening?" Jad cried.

"His Choosing."

"How handsome he looks."

Thayn shook his head. "They don't know any better. It's Vok's spell. He'll erase their memory of it."

A diminutive young woman and her parents entered the Hall of Choosing. They chanted softly and quickly together. Again the room shook and cracks in the face of the wall defined the Fourth Door. Jad stood in front of her.

"Jad, be careful." Thayn worried that their intervention might do more harm than good.

The Fourth Door swung open. The young woman quickly dispatched Jad sideways with a glancing blow, retrieved from her parents several jars of honeydrop and disappeared. The Fourth Door slammed shut. The young woman's parents smiled stupidly after her.

Yara entered the Hall as Thayn vowed, "I have to go after them."

"What's happening?" Yara asked.

"Trea baab caac daad." Thayn spoke slowly with grim resolution. These words sealed the Third Door.

Jad understood him. *"Trea abba acca adda,"* he sadly offered in return. These words opened it.

The incantations, spoken together, would confuse the Third Door and, as a result, the Fourth Door would open. Bravely, without saying goodbye, they chanted.

"Trea abba acca adda."

"Trea baab caac daad."

The Third Door swung wide and shuddered. Confounded, it slammed shut, slanting in its frame. Thayn and Jad expected that, in response, the Fourth Door would open. Thayn prepared himself, ready to spring through it.

The room didn't shake. The wall didn't crack. The Fourth Door didn't appear.

No further pulsation violated the city. Everything was quiet and still. After a moment the remaining Genexus left the Hall of Choosing as if following directions, their faces expressionless.

"Let them go," Jad called to Yara as they passed

her. There was nothing to be done.

"I was at prayer," Yara related. "A storm gathered over the temple. The wind and thunder were deafening. When I awoke, I was in my bed."

"You were distracted," Thayn explained, "to mask the opening of the Fourth Door."

"No," Yara exclaimed.

"How many youth of Kala," Thayn wondered, "did he take with him – this time? Reports of the missing will begin soon, but their parents will remember nothing. It's the work of Vok."

"I've failed them," Yara admitted.

Thayn shook his head, reflective. "Only if we accept their fate. We need to figure out a way to rescue them." He hated his words and looked regretfully at Jad. How easy it would be to give up, but he knew that Jad wouldn't let him. Thayn remembered what Cyrll told him. In Jad's eyes Thayn would never fail.

Other Ministration joined Yara. "Several children have come with their neighbors. They say their parents are ill, and they don't know where their older brothers and sisters are. They're frightened."

Yara glanced at Thayn in sad wonder at all that had come to pass. To the Ministration she replied, "Yes, of course, I'll come at once." She took leave of them.

* Chapter Four *

Thayn returned to the wall next to the Third Door and ran his hand along it. "It's hot."

Jad looked at him intently. "So, what will you do now?"

"Why won't it open for me?" Thayn pounded on the wall. "I need guidance. I know – I'll go to the temple of Kala."

"Of course."

"Will you come with me part of the way?" Thayn added. "There's a place I want you to know."

CHAPTER FIVE
Journey to Vok

The morning air was cool and moist as Thayn and Jad ventured out of the Ring of Eator and into the grasslands. With the return of their powers they were formidable to the eye. They followed a path toward the river, leaving it to arrive upstream of the island city of Tordawn.

The Blue One and a companion waited. Thayn and Jad joined them in the river and they secured the Woodswarder in place. Then, with a sweep and flutter of blue arms and feet, they sliced through the water against the current.

Jad held tightly as they twirled through bubbling rapids and long still pools. Feathery weeds grew on either side of fluid pathways that the Blue Men negotiated with ease.

The sunlight shifted as the river looped. The bank

grew steeper. They passed Tordusk, but Jad and Thayn didn't notice. Everything faded to blue.

Smooth stone reached overhead as they entered a final pool. The water was unequivocally clear. They glided across the Well of Understanding.

The Blue Men somersaulted. Thayn and Jad sailed onto a rocky ledge. The walls of a grotto wrapped around in either direction until, opposite them, they met to form an arch through which the river issued.

Behind Thayn and Jad a cave breached the wall. Water trickled along its floor. Illuminated by a faint light within, the cave tunneled into a spar of the mountains and curved out of sight. At the end of the tunnel was the Diversionary.

Faces surrounded by weedy hair, the Blue Men bobbed in and out of the water. Thayn stood up and bowed his head to them. Jad did the same. The Blue Men sprang through the air and, returning to the water without a splash, disappeared.

Thayn reached out and took Jad by the hand. He smiled. "Come."

They followed the tunnel beyond its curve. It divided to either side. Thayn asked Jad to choose a way. At the next fork the tunnel divided up and down. Thayn showed Jad the water that flowed uphill.

Next, the tunnel divided sideways and the water trickled across the wall. Thayn and Jad stepped gingerly onto it and followed the flow.

They reached the Diversionary. Countless doorways, all in which they stood, opened into it from every angle. Thayn and Jad stepped into empty space. All the doorways, except the one through which they arrived, disappeared. They entered twin domes of pale pink pillars. The domes intersected one another.

Thayn sat on a fallen pillar near the center of one of the domes. "Explore for yourself."

Jad made his way along the smooth wall of warm pink rock, walking away from Thayn. The wall curved back toward Thayn to meet the adjoining dome. Continuing, Jad followed the wall away from Thayn until he approached him for a second time.

"Here I am again."

"Remember you said that," Thayn replied, laughing. "Come and sit. I'm going to the other dome for a moment."

"But – "

"Study the water."

Fallen pillars formed a ring around a center column that reached to the ceiling. Water flowed both up and down the stone. Jad blinked and, seemingly from the column itself, Thayn appeared.

"How did you do that?" Jad asked.

"Jad," Thayn replied with a smile, reaching out to him.

"But – "

"Jad?" A voice called from behind him – Thayn's voice.

Jad turned around. "What – ?" He quickly looked from Thayn who joined them to Thayn who stood beside the column and back again.

"Thayn?" Jad heard what sounded like his own voice. Following Thayn from the other dome Jad saw *himself*.

"What's happening?" he asked, addressing either Thayn.

Thayn by the column replied, "The answer to your question isn't within the scope of my purpose."

Thayn behind him explained, "He's a phantasm. So is Jad behind me."

Jad looked puzzled.

"This way, before I go, we'll have twice the memories of our time together."

"Come to me," invited Thayn by the column.

"Go to him," Thayn behind him urged.

*

How long did Thayn and Jad visit in the Diversionary? Jad wasn't sure. Not only couldn't he keep track of time, he couldn't keep track of which Thayn was Thayn and which him was himself. Was Jad dreaming? No. Whenever he awoke Thayn appeared again from the column. If he roused Thayn at his side, another Jad appeared.

*

The memories that Thayn and Jad shared of their time together in the Diversionary were more than twice over – they were immeasurable. At last Thayn spoke the inevitable words, "I need to go."

Jad nodded solemnly.

They made their way back along the tunnel to the grotto. Thayn advised, "The Blue One will take you as far as Tordawn. The powers of Kala will protect you until you're safely home. Then they'll weaken and it will take you several days to recover."

"I remember." Jad smiled.

Thayn admitted, "I'm saying unnecessary things because I don't want you to leave."

"Let's not make it more difficult." Jad gave Thayn half an embrace. "A gesture of expectation. I'll complete it when you get back."

Thayn reached out to him but, instead, Jad sprang

sideways. He dove into the pool and the Blue One appeared. With a ripple – Jad's ripple – they were gone.

*

Thayn collected his thoughts. He waded into the pool and, with a deep breath, raised his arms over his head. He sank into the Well of Understanding.

The passageway plunged and twisted sideways until, above Thayn, the rock opened to expose another pool. A glow reached down through the water. Thayn swam up into it.

He broke the surface and, with several quick kicks, floated to the edge of the pool and pulled himself out of the water. Thayn stood in a cavern of white crystal, the temple of Kala. Overhead its arches filled with prayers from throughout the land. The crystal walls filled with light that burst free and flew to meet incoming supplications. A number of them lamented the stolen youth whom Vok held hostage. Thayn sympathized with them.

He found the dais in which Jovia had appeared to him the last time that he visited. It was blank. His physical presence, Thayn remembered, didn't guarantee him the attention that he sought. Thayn would need to pray.

He composed his thoughts. Just as he was ready to

begin his prayer he caught a whiff of something familiar. "Here?" Curious, Thayn hurried among the crystals to an opening in the wall. The temple sat on a bluff that, along with several others, had separated from the main body of the land upon impact. Thayn squinted against the bright sunlight to get a better view of the broken neck of Kala.

As every Woodsward learned from his mentor, Kala suffered a hard landing when he fell into the desert. His mighty shoulders, one higher than the other, rested below the broken bluffs. They curved to meet ribbed highlands that, along with the far mountains, contained vast grasslands. Surrounding Kala was nothing but sand and sky except – Thayn sensed on the horizon the presence of a new land. It was Vok.

Thayn's musings were interrupted by another whiff of the same familiar scent. It was unquestionably leafcake. He followed it to discover a makeshift camp just outside the temple walls. Someone Thayn recognized sat at a small fire. "Boz?"

"Thayn?" Boz stood up, his arms opened wide. When Thayn tried to embrace the old man, his arms went right through him. "Is Rykos with you?"

"No."

"All the more leafcake for us, then. Tell me, has a

name been chosen for the baby?"

"I don't think so."

"Don't let them name him or her after me. I was thinking 'Aryk' for a boy and 'Aryka' for a girl. It's a clever name, don't you think? Tell them for me."

"Boz, what are you doing out here?" Thayn gestured toward the temple. "Why aren't you with everyone else?"

"I'm taking a welcome break from eternity. Remember how I used to say 'ether you live or die – '? Well, it's more complicated than that. There are many ways to be dead." Boz sighed and shook his head. "They already have one foot in the Abysm."

"Who do?"

"Jovia and Lor."

"How are they?" Thayn asked.

"Fine, fine. They want to meet up with old friends, I suppose, but I'm in no hurry." He stirred his campfire, mumbling. "Besides, we're all the same in the Archive of Time."

The camp and Boz' leafcake were both illusionary. Thayn wondered, "Are you homesick, Boz?"

"I suppose I am. Come. Lor and Jovia will be upset if they miss your visit."

Thayn retraced his steps into the temple. "I need

help, Boz."

"You've come to the right place."

Thayn concentrated. His prayer leapt into the air and sailed overhead. Two pulses of light burst from a facing wall to intercept his supplication. They settled within the same crystal that, on Thayn's previous visit, served as a dais.

"Thayn's here," Boz told their images.

"I'm aware of it," Lor squeaked.

Jovia smiled. "Thayn, we're glad to see you."

"I wanted to say hello."

"That's not why you've come all this way, is it, to say hello?" Lor demanded. "Speak."

Thayn frowned. "More youth of Kala have been abducted. You've heard all the prayers on their behalf, haven't you?"

"Tell us everything you know – "

"And you," Thayn laughed, interrupting, "will tell me more, I know."

"Begin." Even in death Lor controlled the conversation.

Thayn related his news of the High Summit and the reopening of the Fourth Door. Jovia, Lor and Boz exchanged several glances as Thayn described events. He concluded with a question. "The Fourth Door – it wouldn't open for me. Why?"

Lor's voice was unusually shrill. "We prevented it."

"But I – "

"Our intuition has been sound. The consequences of your success, we've learned, wouldn't have been as you intended."

"What then?"

"If you had opened the Fourth Door by con-founding the Third Door – both Kala and Vok have done so – you would have fallen to the desert as a new land."

Thayn didn't consider the various implications of Lor's news. Instead he wanted to know, "How is the Fourth Door opening now?"

"Vok's spell. The words are communicated by a pulsation and repeated by the parents of the Chosen."

"If," Thayn wondered, "I'm in the Hall of Choos-ing when the Fourth Door opens from within, can I pass through it the way I am?"

"Evidently."

"Then that's what I'll do."

"Thayn – ?" Jovia had been a teacher and Thayn immediately knew from her tone that he was wrong in his thinking. "What are the chances of being in the

Hall of Choosing at the right time? And if Vok senses you, what then?"

"You're right," Thayn admitted. "What'll I do?"

"We must think harder," Lor squeaked.

"We must learn more," Jovia added.

"You could walk," Boz suggested.

They all looked at Boz. "What?" Jovia exclaimed.

"But the desert doesn't sustain life," Lor objected. "He'd perish."

"Unless – " Being neither a Woodsward nor Ministrant, Boz was wise in ways that Woodswarder and Ministration weren't.

"Unless what?" Jovia asked.

"Something I've learned about the berries might protect him."

"Tell us what you know," Lor demanded.

"There's one here, an old Genexus, who knows quite a bit about baking, and grains and berries. He described to me a cake that's quite tasty, although dry. 'Dry *as* the desert,' in fact, were his words. 'And *for* the desert – ' he went on. You see, people once journeyed there, he told me. 'Once upon a time – '"

"Enough. Tell us of the berries and what the old soul means." Lor spoke impatiently.

Jovia interceded, suggesting, "We'll hear more of

your friend's story another time."

"What color are the berries?" Lor asked.

"Black, I suppose. He spoke of berries that were dry on a bush that was dead."

Thayn interrupted, "On my last visit a bush grew here by the dais."

"A bush of powerful berries," Jovia noted. "Is it still there, Thayn?"

Thayn reached down and held up a withered bush. Its branches were laden with sprigs of shriveled berries.

"They've lost their color," Lor objected. "How do you interpret the berries?"

"You don't," Boz explained. "They've lost whatever powers they previously had. Now they'll fortify Thayn for a journey across the desert."

"Must he bake them into a cake?"

"It would be tastier that way, of course," Boz considered, "but he only needs to swallow them."

"And their effect?"

"I was told the dried berries will lighten his feet and level his way."

"But the desert is flat," Thayn observed.

"The desert is enigmatic and Vok will defend himself."

"Yes," Boz affirmed, "Those are as the old soul described. Eat them when you are upon the desert and only in response to need."

"What need?"

"As with the powers of Kala, you'll know what to do when the need arises," Lor reminded Thayn.

Jovia asked, "Are there other provisions required for such a journey?"

"I have my cloak for protection, and hardbread and waterfruit."

"The cloak will shield you from the sun, but it will be very hot. You won't want the hardbread, so there's no point in carrying it. The berries, you see, will make you thirsty, not hungry, and if you can't find food once you have reached Vok, that will be the least of your troubles. You'll need more waterfruit. It grows on the far side of the bluff." These were Boz' words. Jovia and Lor looked at him with new respect.

Jovia reached a hand out to Thayn. From it emanated a spark that broke through the dais and swirled about his forehead. It was her blessing. "Go."

Thayn nodded to Lor and Jovia. He attempted to hug Boz a last time but, within his embrace, the old man faded to a pulse of light that flew to the dais. Boz reappeared beside the others. They waved at Thayn as he left the temple.

*

A rift in the bluff protected a patch of waterfruit from the afternoon sun. Thayn climbed into it. After harvesting more fruit than his sack would carry, Thayn wove the vine into a net. He fashioned another receptacle in which to carry the rest.

The day was nearly spent. Thayn decided to spend the night there. He made a camp similar to Boz'. As Thayn emptied his sack of hardloaf he was delighted to find a leafcake that was real – and delicious.

*

The next morning Thayn readied himself. He returned to the portion of the bluff that faced Vok and studied his surroundings. The sun was bright. Its burn, as Boz noted, would be worse than its heat.

Thayn pulled his cloak around him. The waterfruit were heavy, but Thayn worried that his load would lighten too soon. He chose the gentlest slope that he could find. "Oh," he cried as he lost his footing and tumbled to the desert floor.

Thayn sat up and rubbed his shoulder. It ached. With a grunt, he returned to his feet.

The world reeled.

The desert, which lay perfectly flat as he sat, inclined sharply as he stood. Fearing that he would slip backwards, Thayn reached forward to steady himself and fell to his knees. The desert became level again.

What was this? Again he tried to stand up and the desert tilted. He fell. Bewitchment – already? His journey had barely begun.

"The berries," he remembered. He plucked one from a sprig in his sack and chewed it. His mouth grew dry. He pulled out a waterfruit and sucked on it.

Thayn immediately felt the effect of the berry. He stood up. Now the desert descended. He took easy steps. The sand seemed spongy underfoot.

He departed Kala.

*

The land of Vok appeared in the distance. Waves of heat that rose in the expanse between it and Thayn obscured his view. The surrounding desert faded from gray to blue and, in places, shimmered silvery black.

Thayn made good progress until, without warning, the desert ascended again. Thayn sank to the sand, grabbing his sack. He swallowed another berry and sucked on another waterfruit. The desert descended and Thayn continued.

*

The sun burned brighter. Step by step, Vok grew

nearer. The berry wore off more quickly this time. Again, the world tilted.

Thayn sat for a moment. His mouth was so dry. He didn't want another berry, but he knew that he had no choice.

There was no wind, not even an occasional breeze. The day grew hotter. Something heavy seemed to push down on Thayn. A simultaneous surge of exhaustion swept over him.

He swallowed another berry. Slowly the desert descended again and he continued on his way. Another waterfruit wasn't enough to satisfy Thayn's thirst, but he needed to conserve them. His throat parched and he felt increasingly itchy.

*

The cycle repeated itself. The sand lost its springiness and the desert ascended. Thayn fell. Another berry and the desert descended. Another waterfruit. Waves of weariness washed over Thayn as the desert angled up and down. Another berry. More waterfruit. So itchy and dry.

The interval of the cycle grew shorter. How many more berries would it take? Thayn was almost out of waterfruit. He imagined faint cries in the distance. The crying of children.

*

Thayn lay flat on his back on the desert floor. The sun blazed overhead. He tried to move, but something prevented him. It pressed down upon him, an invisible force. Thayn felt his consciousness ebb.

A power, yes, as Lor – or Boz – had suggested. It was Vok. His energy pinned him to the sand, preventing him from regaining his feet, obstructing his progress. "I give up – oh."

Thayn surrendered himself to defeat until a trait that he shared with his mother, one that usually alerted him when things seemed too good to be true, led him to the opposite conclusion. The present situation was too *bad* to be true. Facts that he had learned as Vok's agent in the Forbidden Room returned to him. His predicament was just a perception. The desert was level. The sun was itself. It was a delusion that defeated him. Only, perhaps, the crying that he heard was real.

Thayn tried to muster his strength. He rolled onto his stomach and pushed himself up with his arms. His elbows gave away and he smacked into the sand.

He rolled over again. Bright sunlight blinded him. Through his closed lids he saw pink. His consciousness wavered.

Pink. As in the Diversionary. "Thayn?"

"Jad – ?" he attempted.

"Wake up. You have to continue." Was it possible? Did Jad really stand over him? "You can't stay here. Eat these."

Thayn looked up. All he could manage was a dry whisper. "No." A berry pressed against his lips.

"Just one," Jad urged.

Thayn swallowed the berry and sucked on the last waterfruit.

"Another," Jad repeated, "another." One by one the remaining berries disappeared.

Thayn stood. The desert declined in front of him. "Hurry." The land of Vok grew nearer.

After only moments the slope shifted again. Thayn struggled with every step. The desert rose as if a wall. Thayn slammed against it, held fast by the will of Vok. Jad called to him, "Hurry. There are no more berries. There are no more waterfruit. You must –

" – not fail." The voice began as Jad's but finished as his own.

With an ultimate burst of effort Thayn climbed up the desert and scrambled onto a bony finger of land. He collapsed and the world grew black.

PART TWO

CHAPTER SIX
Nicca

"Oh-h," Thayn groaned. He lay outstretched on a finger of earth that clenched the sand. It was hard and crusty. Behind him the desert reached away into the distance.

At first only his eyes moved. His body ached. Slowly Thayn remembered where he was. His next thought was of the stolen youth of Kala, those whom he came to rescue. He turned his head.

It hurt.

The gritty slope rose to a crooked limb of land – the arm of Vok. It was repugnant to Thayn, but he lacked the strength to rise.

His sack rested uphill of him, empty. Between it and Thayn was a berry. A last berry. Had Jad left it for him?

Jad. Had he really been there?

* Chapter Six *

Thayn tried to push himself up, unsuccessfully. "Oh-h," he groaned again, unable to move.

The ground trembled. The berry hopped. It rolled toward Thayn and he reached out his tongue.

This berry was as dark as the others had been but, far from dry, it was plump and juicy. Thayn bit it and it burst. He felt warmth travel through him and swirl around in his head.

The ground beneath him was no longer offensive to his touch. Thayn sat up. He rubbed his head and looked around him.

His previous thinking slipped away as his strength grew. With it came another feeling both familiar and unfamiliar. It involved something that he wanted – he didn't know what it was yet – but he had to get it.

Thayn stood. He felt replete with purpose. He no longer considered the stolen youth of Kala and his mission to be –

"What – ?" In a shadow of scrub he saw a pair of eyes. Someone – or something – was smiling at him. It was gone with a scramble of feet.

Thayn made chase without thinking twice. He ran up the crumbly slant of earth and along a ridge. He watched for movement in the brush, but the uneven terrain hindered his pursuit.

The limb along which Thayn ran and the rest of the land met at an awkward angle, as if something once right had been broken. Beyond its high shoulder another formation abutted the nascent land. Earlier, from mountains now distant, Owan had seen in its features the face of Vok.

A broad expanse descended before Thayn and rose again in the distance. Its length twisted out of sight. Everything was crooked and felt uncomfortable.

Whatever Thayn was chasing scampered away.

The land was an odd contradiction of generation and corruption. Water misted from fiery fissures that cracked its surface. It stank.

Bramble grew in isolated patches, withered roots held together by broken clumps of soil, tender tips a sickly green. Brittle stalks were laden with dark ripe berries. Dry grasses sprouted brightly colored burrs. Such was the stubble of Vok.

The ground trembled. Thayn held out a hand to steady himself. Behind him the limb of land that had delivered him from the desert slipped away. The earth beneath him buckled. Thayn squatted, pushing against the ground with his fingertips as if riding a piece of it, until the shaking stopped. At last, the land evened out.

The bramble shook. Thayn looked into it. Two

bright eyes blinked and were gone.

Thayn hurried after them – after it – again. He wanted whatever it was that he chased. Bush after bush shook, mocking his desire. Thayn caught fleeting glimpses of bright eyes, white teeth and a taunting smile. He followed them deep into the stubble.

*

Above the high shoulder of the land a twisted isthmus led to the cliff in which Owan had seen from afar the scowl of Vok. From it rose a temple of black crystal and within it, at a dais, stood Laerl. White blond hair framed his handsome face.

He was growing more powerful, more muscular. His homespun tunic hung from him in tatters. Behind him on the stone floor sat empty jars of honeydrop.

He munched a mottled berry. Laerl was taking his lessons. He concentrated, vanished and reappeared.

"Good," cackled Vok's voice from within the dais. "You'll be ready soon."

*

A small gray shape backed between two bushes. Thayn was waiting for it. He had tricked it by throwing stones in one direction and making his way around the other. The creature was more than an animal but less than a man.

Thayn grabbed for it. It bit his leg and scurried away. Behind him came a peal of laughter.

"You'll never catch it like that," rang a high, clear voice. Hopping on one foot and holding the other leg below the knee, Thayn turned around to discover a young woman. "Did it bite you badly?"

"No," Thayn replied.

"Pity." She continued on her way.

She was about his age, Thayn thought. She might have been pretty, but it was hard to tell. Frizzy brown hair was matted against her head. Her face and her tattered, faded gown were smeared with dirt.

"What was it? What bit me?"

She didn't stop.

"Wait. Where are you going?" Thayn tore a strip of cloth from his cloak. "Who are you? Wait."

She didn't.

Thayn tied the strip around his wound. He limped after her through the stubble of Vok. The passing bushes grew greener and taller. "Who are you? Why won't you wait?"

Trees emerged through the bramble. Thayn followed the young woman in and out of several woods. He lagged behind her as the trees thickened. Finally Thayn decided that he would be no worse off without her. "I won't go another step unless you wait."

He sat and tended to his leg. The bleeding soon subsided. He cleaned the wound with spit and tore another strip from his cloak.

"Here," rang that high, clear voice again.

Thayn looked up.

The young woman had a wide forehead and oval eyes. She handed him a small, wrinkled fruit. "It will heal your wound. It's like greenfruit, but nasty, and it stinks." Her lips receded with a smile.

Thayn dressed his leg. "Thank you. Why didn't you stop?" he asked when he was done.

"I wanted to see how long you'd follow me."

Thayn laughed. He thought that she was joking. "Who are you?"

"Pick a name." Her expression hardened and she tossed her head. "It doesn't matter. I don't care."

"Where do you come from, what city? And really, what's your name?"

Her chin quivered. "Nicca," she sobbed, rushing into his arms and hugging him.

"I'm Thayn." As she looked over his shoulder her expression changed.

"Come." She pushed herself away from him and adjusted her ragged gown. Then she hurried away in a new direction. Thayn followed her again.

"Where are we going?" he asked repeatedly.

They entered a little woods. At its center, tucked within the wall of a small clearing, was a smaller hollow. It was Nicca's home. She gestured for Thayn to sit on a pile of leaves.

"Where are the others?" he asked.

"Who?" Nicca replied.

"The others who came with you."

"Nobody came with me."

"The youth of Kala," Thayn explained, "the young men and women stolen by Vok from cities throughout the land."

"Vok?"

"He tricked you. You thought you attended your Choosing. Instead Vok brought you here."

Nicca looked at Thayn oddly. "Youth of Kala?"

"Your stones were thrown. You're not a child anymore."

She grabbed his face and kissed him. "No, I'm not."

Surprised, Thayn leaned away, flushing. "Where are the others?" he repeated.

"In the Great Clearing, some of them." Abruptly Nicca left the little hollow. Thayn followed her.

Across the stubble grew greater woods. They entered the largest one of them. Nicca made her way
stealthily through the trees, trunk by trunk, clearly expecting Thayn to do the same. Ahead the trees thinned
and Thayn saw a number of young men and women.
Their attire, once colorful, was as faded and tattered as
Nicca's. "Don't let them see you or they'll kill you."

"Is this – ?"

"Hush," Nicca whispered, scolding him. She retraced her steps now, backing away from the Great
Clearing, again trunk by trunk. Thayn remained a moment to watch the others. He felt something unexpected that came from the clearing. Or did it come
from himself? It was a sense of shame. Among the
youth of Kala he saw creatures. They were yellow and
their teeth were pointed.

Thayn retreated after Nicca. He lost sight of her
several times as she disappeared into adjacent woods.
He called to her, "Wait. I want to come with you," but
she didn't stop until she was home again. Luckily,
Thayn remembered the way.

*

"What took you so long?" Nicca asked. "And
what's that?"

Thayn dropped from the trees outside her hollow

carrying an armful of vines. He asked her questions as he wove them together. "Tell me, what do you know of this land? Exactly who's here?"

"Horrible people." Nicca watched Thayn weave.

"How many of them?"

"Too many." She pointed at the vines. "What – ?"

"Are they all in the Great Clearing?"

"No. There are many clearings. Those who live in them will kill you, too." Her curiosity grew too much for her and she asked crossly, "What are you doing?"

"Weaving these together. I'll show you when I'm done. Why would they want to kill me, or you?"

Nicca considered. "Because we're threats."

"Threats? How?"

"We're threats to anyone who wants to rule the clearings."

"Rule them? Can't the clearings be shared?"

"I don't want to share." Nicca sulked.

Thayn finished his work in silence. Completed, he had woven the vines together into a web. "To hang high up in the branches," he explained.

"Why?"

"It'll be my station."

"Your station is here with me."

"No."

"It's not fair. I found you. You're going to be up *there*?" Nicca asked, squinting against the sunlight that flickered between the leaves. She sobbed, "Why don't you treat me the same as the others?"

"I'm not like them," Thayn explained. He leapt into a tree and climbed it quickly, securing his weaving high above in the canopy.

Nicca watched as the green web stretched over her hollow. After Thayn appeared to be done and nothing more happened, she grew impatient. "Aren't you coming down?"

"I'm at your call," Thayn shouted, "but first I need some sleep. And when I wake up, I'll need food and water." There was something else that Thayn wanted. He felt it all around him, but he didn't know what it was.

*

The next morning a blue sky dappled with green leaves and golden light offered Thayn comfort. Then a foul odor came with the wind. He remembered where he was.

He climbed down from the trees and dropped into the hollow. Nicca wasn't there. On a table fashioned out of branches sat dark berries, waterfruit and stalks of a variety that Thayn recognized from Eator – they weren't his favorite, but they were edible.

He ate. The stalks were stringy and the waterfruit was dry. The berries, at least, were plump and almost tasty. With them came immediate warmth that traveled through Thayn. His surroundings seemed to welcome him. Also came a sense of wariness. He wondered where Nicca was. He thought about the Great Clearing and contradictory feelings swept over him.

One feeling was desire. For what? The youth of Kala were there. Why should Nicca rule it? The Great Clearing was rightfully his, wasn't it? After all, he had come all this way.

The other feeling that Thayn experienced was one of unworthiness.

Something moved in the underbrush beneath the trees at the edge of the hollow. Thayn saw faces again. One was gray and the other was yellow. They smiled at him and Thayn's feelings intensified.

Nicca returned and the faces disappeared.

"You found the food I set out for you," she observed, acknowledging her own hospitality. "It's horrible, but it's the best I can find."

"Where did you get it?"

"From the Great Clearing. They didn't want it and threw it away. You see, things are better there."

With her words the first feeling revisited Thayn. He coveted the Great Clearing. In the bushes he saw the gray face again.

Then the other face appeared and the second feeling returned. He was ashamed of himself. "There they are again. Those creatures."

"Where?"

"In the brush. Don't you see them?"

"Describe them."

"The first is gray – "

"The one that bit you."

"Yes. The second is yellow – "

"No," she interrupted. "Where?"

"There." Thayn pointed.

She ran in its direction. "Go away," she screamed.

The yellow creature disappeared. Thayn no longer felt the unworthiness that it seemed to provoke.

Nicca returned. "If it bothers you again, let me know."

"What are they?"

"They're peculiar to this place, I think. Creatures of the land. Some of them are useful. Others are to be avoided." She peered into the shadows. "That's what Laerl told Ayan."

"Who?"

"Ayan – the leader of the Great Clearing, at least for now."

"No, the other – "

"Laerl? He *was* there, but he's gone."

"Where?" Thayn grabbed Nicca by the shoulders.

She closed her eyes and puckered her lips as if expecting Thayn to kiss her. When nothing happened she opened her eyes again and, after a shrug, replied, "I don't know."

"I need to speak to Ayan."

"He'll kill you."

"I'll figure out how to prevent that," Thayn replied.

He and Nicca exchanged looks. "I *can* prevent it," she vowed.

They regarded each other differently. Each took on a new role in the other's plans. "How?"

"If you help me."

"Help you what?" Thayn asked.

"Regain the Great Clearing. It was mine. I'm its rightful leader. It was taken from me by force, by Ayan. I want it back." Her manner became matter-of-fact. She would do whatever was necessary, Thayn could tell, to achieve her goal.

"I see. I'll help you, but I need information."

"What do you want to know?"

Thayn asked Nicca about the size of the Great Clearing. It was no bigger than Tordawn. He asked Nicca about its fortifications and guards. There were no stations. "But Ayan has many who work to defend him. We have to sneak in somehow," Nicca proposed, "surprise Ayan and kill him."

"The trees," Thayn prompted her.

"What?" Nicca asked.

"Tell me about the trees."

CHAPTER SEVEN
Leok

In the middle of the Great Clearing, within a crude shack, sat Ayan. Both he and Laerl were from Yutor. Thayn would recognize Ayan from his recent adventures there, but he didn't know Ayan by name.

He sat at a table with several ragged young men, his captains. They all had white blond hair. Their conversation concerned the growing number that they held captive. There were too many of them to control.

"We'll pick one," Ayan decided, "and make an example of him – or her – in front of everybody. The rest will do as they're told."

Unctuous subordinates arrived with various foodstuffs that they gathered from the woods, fruit, mushrooms, berries and stalks. A thin young man with a broken nose offered bread that he had baked.

"Horrible," one of the captains complained.

"It's too sweet," Ayan hissed. He threw his bread at its baker. The others did the same. "What's your name again?"

"Leok," the hapless baker replied, combing the crumbs out of his stringy hair.

Ayan smiled, looking from him to his captains and back again. "Because the bread you baked displeases us – Leok – you are a candidate for our plan." Leok smiled in return, not knowing what Ayan meant, and Ayan's captains smiled, too.

*

It was almost morning. A full moon offered Thayn good light. He and Nicca made their way through the trees surrounding the Great Clearing. A breeze rustling the leaves offered them protection from the ear. "Perfect," Thayn whispered.

Suddenly he was up a tree, high up, and then in the next. Soon he reached the Great Clearing. He carried with him a coiled vine that was attached to a short pole of wood.

Thayn descended to a lower branch and threw the pole across the clearing to an opposite tree. It lodged. He pulled the vine taut and tied it. Hand over hand, he positioned himself above the shack in which Ayan slept.

*

Ayan's memories of the attack on Yutor were still raw. In vivid nightmares he remembered screams and shouts. A dark shape pulled his father out the door. Ayan jumped through a window and hurried to his side. It was too late. His father lay in pieces. Above him Ayan heard hideous laughter.

*

Thayn broke through the roof of Ayan's shack and dropped to the floor, calling the young man by name. "Ayan?"

"No-o," Ayan cried, looking up at his worst nightmare. He easily imagined Vok in the moonlight standing over him. Sobbing, Ayan surrendered.

Thayn snarled, attempting to appear terrible, but he needn't have bothered. At this point he recognized the young man with white blond hair. "Aren't you from Yutor?" This was too easy.

"Yes."

"Close your eyes." He tied Ayan's hands behind his back with vine and blindfolded him with another strip that he tore from his cloak. "Who's next to you in power?"

"I have – captains. They help me keep – "

"From what cities are they?" Thayn interrupted.

"I – I don't remember."

"Do they wear gray?"

"No."

"How do you call them?"

"I whistle."

"Do it."

Ayan pursed his lips. No sound came out. He wetted them. A weak note emerged.

"Again."

His whistle was clearer now, three notes, the second higher than the others.

"Again."

Ayan's captains hurried into the shack from the surrounding woods. One by one they stopped short. Thayn held a knife to Ayan's throat.

Thayn warned them, "I'll kill him if you come any closer. Beg them," he whispered to Ayan in case anyone remained unconvinced.

"Please, don't," Ayan cried. Begrudgingly, with many a sideways glance, his captains complied.

"Tell your friends about me."

Ayan recounted Vok's assault on his city. The details were terrifying. His captains stepped away from Thayn as Ayan completed his tale.

"For the moment I've more use for you alive than

dead," Thayn told Ayan, grabbing a wooden pike that hung by the door. He pushed Ayan, still bound and blindfolded, out of the shack and through the Great Clearing.

Ayan's captains and several spectators followed them. Thayn shoved Ayan into the stubble of Vok, taking a few steps after him. "Tell everyone you meet about me, my power and violence.

"Warn others not to cross me or my path. Or – " he took Ayan's hand and guided it up the pike to the sharpened point " – your head will decorate this. Now run.

"Run until you can't hear my voice. Then you can figure out how to free your hands and your eyes. Go."

Ayan ran, stumbling, and Thayn laughed.

He whirled around, the pike out in front of him. One of Ayan's captains had advanced, but stopped short. Thayn positioned the point of the pike against the young man's tattered tunic. "I respect allegiance – once. Provoke me again and you're dead." He pressed the pike just enough to score a line of blood across the young man's chest.

Thayn called into the trees. Nicca appeared and joined them. Ayan's captains spat, cursing her.

"Aren't you happy to see me again, brothers?" she

taunted them. Without waiting for them to respond she implored of Thayn, "Let me kill them now."

"No."

"Then tie them up and keep a close eye on them. They're dangerous."

"I will." He called after Ayan, "Keep running."

"Help us," Nicca encouraged a growing crowd of spectators. She bound the first captain's hands behind his back and told an eager volunteer to do the same with the next. She added, "I remember you. Have you learned to bake bread sweet as I instructed?"

"Yes," Leok replied, an odd smile upon his lips.

Thayn, Nicca and Leok escorted Ayan's captains back to the shack. Nicca bound them to its outside wall, leaving Leok in charge of them, and went inside.

The shack was originally hers. She reclaimed it, removing its contents and throwing them at Ayan's captains' feet. "I must cleanse my space of this filth."

Thayn climbed into the trees and brought back an armful of vine. He told Nicca, "You can rule the clearing and I'll protect it." He would weave a new web to hang overhead.

Nicca ignored him, mumbling something to herself about friends. She slipped away as Thayn worked and didn't return until after he had finished. He secured his weaving in the treetops over the shack.

*

Nicca's friends, unlike Ayan's captains, were a diverse group. They consisted of two young men, one tall and the other short, and three women, skinny, squat and sallow. There was an ugly verbal exchange between Ayan's captains and Nicca's friends as they followed her into the shack.

"Thayn – ? Where is he?" The shack was empty. Without warning he dropped from above through the hole in the roof. One of Nicca's friends sprang upon him, knocking him to the ground.

"No, *no.*" Nicca called, her oval eyes disappearing above her cheeks as she suppressed a smile. "This is Thayn. He's here to – *protect* – us." She looked away, trying not to laugh.

"Hello." Thayn waved at Nicca's friends.

Nicca looked back with an expression of forced gravity. "You'll do his bidding and serve him as you would me. Is that understood?"

"Yes," they agreed. Thayn nodded in return, smiling good-naturedly. He asked them questions about the Great Clearing.

Ayan hadn't been in power long. His captains had moved into positions that already existed, positions created by their predecessors, now their successors. Nicca's friends would simply resume their previous duties.

There were two significant exceptions. One was Thayn. Nicca repeated that he would be in charge of their protection, although whenever Thayn looked the other way she rolled her eyes.

The other exception was the prisoners. "Ah-h," Thayn heard one of them cry.

He followed Nicca outside. Leok had forced several of them into a compromising position. Around them a crowd lingered, laughing.

Thayn pulled Leok away from the captains. "Why would you do that to them?" he asked.

The crowd protested. Within it, with bright eyes and sharp teeth, stood small creatures of various colors. They held sprigs of plump dark berries. They were the answer to Thayn's question, but he didn't yet understand it.

"To humiliate them," Leok explained. He tugged on his stringy hair. "They humiliated me."

Thayn wondered how this could be. These young men and women, educated in the ways of Kala, were no better than Outcasts. "You would do better to practice baking your bread. Now go." Thayn pushed Leok away. The crowd murmured, anticipating a fight.

Nicca stepped forward. "Wait. I assigned him this duty."

"I unassign him."

Nicca stared at Thayn. He returned her gaze. The crowd regarded them both. Nobody except Ayan had ever challenged Nicca. She blinked. "As you wish." With her acquiescence Thayn felt new powers visit him. So began the reign of Nicca and Thayn over the Great Clearing in the land of Vok.

*

Thayn prodded Ayan's captains up to his web high over the clearing. Frightened by the height, they sat in its middle. None of them dared move. In an adjacent tree Thayn built himself a cradle.

Nicca returned to power easily. Her friends were strong and vengeful. Thayn and Ayan's captains, as her potential challengers, cancelled one another out.

Thayn spent the majority of his time reclining in his cradle, eating plump, dark berries and exploring the thoughts that they provoked. He watched the captains. What would he do with them?

This was a new situation. Thayn was accustomed to the company of men in trees and, by the stones, he knew that the captains were of age. Thayn studied them one by one, wondering for each of them which of the Doors of Choosing would have opened.

Could they tell? Could Thayn?

He wanted to test the extent of his powers without betraying his strength. He concentrated on the little finger of one of the captains. It twitched at Thayn's command.

*

Thayn and Nicca met daily. He asked her about the land. She truly knew nothing, he decided. He conferred with Nicca's friends who begrudged him little help, and with the captains. By the colors worn at their Choosings he tried to find someone from every city.

How many youth had come with them? As Thayn listened, he calculated at least double the number of those in the Great Clearing were collected elsewhere.

Nicca shared with Thayn little daily business. Instead she flattered him and attempted to flirt. When he refused her solicitations she asked, "Why do you reject me?"

Nothing with Nicca was as it seemed. From the trees above her shack Thayn listened to her meetings. Her invitations were disingenuous. Attempts to curry Thayn's favor were simple manipulation. Among her friends she belittled him as something to cajole.

Duplicity – multiplicity – made Nicca a potential threat. She failed to appreciate, however, the sensitivity of Thayn's hearing. Upon a review of her intent, Thayn resolved to play by her rules – and win. He would gain the most, he decided, by leaving.

*

"I intend to explore the land," Thayn announced during his next audience with Nicca and her friends.

"What?" It wasn't her idea, so she disparaged it. "What purpose is there in that?"

"I'll discover the other clearings, their numbers and defenses."

"We don't care about them."

"Do we wait until they attack us?" Thayn asked.

Nicca frowned.

Thayn continued, "Also, I'll seek out resources. There's much we need."

"Nonsense."

Thayn knew Nicca's mind. His proposal wasn't according to her plan, so it was, at best, an inconvenience. Although she didn't value Thayn, she considered him a risk. Her best defense against him was to make sure that he did nothing at all.

She offered a list of reasons why he shouldn't go, including, "It's too dangerous."

"I'll be careful."

"But you're needed here."

"To do what? I do nothing."

"But I'll miss you if you go."

"You'll *what*?" Thayn laughed derisively.

Nicca turned away and tossed her head. She could think of no other objections. Then she remembered Ayan's captains. "Who will guard the prisoners?"

Thayn smiled. "I'm taking them with me. We'll leave first thing in the morning."

*

That night Nicca called Leok to her. "Thayn – do you hate him?"

Leok looked at her curiously. He quickly guessed correctly, "Yes."

Nicca smiled. "Good. He intends to leave in the morning. Follow him. Do whatever you want with Ayan's scum, but kill Thayn."

*

The sun rose red in a cloudy sky. With his pike Thayn prodded Ayan's captains, shackled, in front of him out of the Great Clearing. He guided them carefully through the stubble of Vok to the nearest woods.

They sat among the trees. Thayn appeared to fall into a trance. Ever convincing, it was never so deep that Thayn couldn't check his captives' restlessness with a sudden start. At last he announced, "I knew it would be so."

Ayan's captains looked at him expectantly.

Thayn addressed them, "Special powers have come to me in response to need. I'll set you free and you'll remember I've done so.

"Collect everyone from the other clearings. I want no one overlooked. Make them strong."

They regarded Thayn with mixed expressions.

Thayn touched a fingertip to his forehead and extended the palm of his other hand in the direction of Ayan's captains. They flinched as his thoughts filled their minds. They heard his unspoken words.

Thayn continued silently, "In the near future, at my signal, you'll bring your followers to the Great Clearing. We'll overpower Nicca and rule together."

Ayan's captains would obey. They stood. Thayn released them from their bonds.

"But first – " Thayn spoke aloud again, pointing into the woods " – get *him*."

Leok dropped from a nearby tree and scrambled away.

CHAPTER EIGHT
Ways of the Great Clearing

Leok was no match for Ayan's captains. "Don't hurt him," Thayn commanded. "I want him."

They brought him back screaming in fear.

Thayn tied a rope around Leok's neck. "Now go," Thayn ordered Ayan's captains. They hastened away in different directions.

Leok crouched as far away from Thayn as the rope would allow and averted his gaze. He was thin, but he wasn't frail, Thayn noted. Despite an unmistakable expression of malice that played upon Leok's face, there was a look of intelligence to him. He asked, "What will you do to me?"

"You're not what you seem to be," Thayn observed.

"What do I seem to be?"

"Harmless."

Leok threw back his head and laughed. Amusement didn't become him, pointing his chin and sharpening his cheeks.

"You won't kill me, though," Thayn added. "Let's go."

"Where?"

"Come." Thayn pulled on the rope. Leok resisted and Thayn pulled harder. Leok stumbled forward and Thayn pushed him against the trunk of the nearest tree. "Climb, then."

"What?" Leok's eyes grew wide as he looked up, unable to disguise his fear.

"You were in a tree earlier, weren't you, spying on us?"

"On the bottom branch – only to hide. I've never climbed – *up* – a tree."

Thayn tied the end of Leok's rope around his own waist. "I'll teach you, but only if you go first." Leok clumsily pulled himself up into the tree and Thayn followed him. Between branches, terrified, he hugged the tapering trunk. Thayn called out directions to him, and words of encouragement.

The wind stirred. "I'll fall," Leok cried.

Thayn pulled on the rope around Leok's neck. "You won't fall far."

* Chapter Eight *

Crouching, they walked along a branch that arched to meet a neighboring tree. With a hop they continued into a next tree, making their way with growing ease through the woods.

Several youth of Kala huddled in a little clearing outside a dilapidated structure. One of Ayan's captains would visit them, Thayn thought to himself. He and Leok skirted the clearing and dropped out of the trees on the opposite side. They continued across the stubble of Vok to the next woods.

"This place is familiar," Leok observed. Saplings protected an outcrop of rock. A smooth wall of stone rippled like a curtain. Thayn inspected it.

Berry bushes grew underfoot. Thayn sensed special powers here and predicted, "This would be an important place someday," his voice distant.

Leok watched him. "You aren't like the others."

Thayn sat next to him. "Tell me of Ayan. And Nicca."

"I don't like them."

"No?"

"None of them."

"An Outcast?" Thayn wondered aloud.

"What?"

"An Outcast is someone who doesn't love." Thayn

touched Leok's cheek. "Do you?"

They camped that night upon the outcrop. Leok had never eaten such berries as grew there. Some were white, part of every Choosing. Thayn surmised that Leok would have been a Woodsward. He taught him some of their ways.

*

They explored the land. Thayn had woven himself and Leok crude leggings. He warned Leok to watch for rats, but there wasn't food enough, Thayn guessed, to support them. There were burrs, though, and their leggings protected them.

Thayn was interested in the river. It was broad across the stubble and took half the morning to reach. Disappointingly, the land of Vok was dry and only a nasty trickle of water traveled the rocky riverbeds. There were no Blue Men.

In the distance a hillock extended from rounded peaks. Steam escaped from it. Squinting, Leok asked, "What's that?"

Thayn recognized the formation and imagined the Diversionary of Vok. "You don't want to know."

The greater part of their journey began. They hastily forded the foul river and continued until, after it made a great loop, they forded the river again. Thayn was interested in the mountains. From the edge of a lake of scum he scrutinized the steep and rocky slopes. Trees grew in the higher crags. Everywhere else was dotted with black. Leok sniffed at the wind and grimaced. "It's so sour."

"Don't breathe it," Thayn warned. He shook his head. There would be no Green Men, either.

Thayn and Leok located all the inhabitable clearings in the land of Vok. Many of them had already been cleared by Ayan's captains. Several clearings were visited as Thayn and Leok watched.

One captain assembled those whom he captured around their former leaders. He tormented them, embarrassing them as Leok had Ayan's captains. Thayn whispered quick words. The captain recoiled from his captives in pain. Leok looked at Thayn in wonder.

In another clearing they watched a captain and his army arrive. At his command they spread themselves among the trees in a circle. Those inside the clearing ran one way, then another, surprised repeatedly as the army tightened around them like a net. They looked as if they were children at play, but their fear was genuine. At last they merged together into a single group. The captain snarled at them and they obeyed. He ordered them to rough quarters.

"This captain – isn't he just as cruel as the other?" Leok asked Thayn.

"This captain uses force to *get* what he wants. The other used force *after* he got it."

Leok considered Thayn's words as they left the woods. "How many more are there?"

"Let me check." Thayn held a hand to the side of his head and reached out in thought. He could sense the youth of Kala. "Ayan's captains have found them all –

" – except – " Thayn stared between the shoulders of Vok and closed his eyes " – Laerl – I can feel him."

*

They returned to the outcrop. Thayn and Leok ate waterfruit and berries. Thayn hopped into a tree and from a branch chinned himself.

"What are you doing?" Leok asked.

"Exercise. I need to stay strong." He raised his legs to form a right angle with his torso.

"Tell me about your powers."

"What do you want to know?" Thayn asked.

"Why don't you use them to stay strong?"

"They come and go with need."

"Who decides the need?"

"What good questions you ask, Leok. Sometimes I

do."

"Who else?"

"Friends. Friends of Kala."

"There are other powers," Leok whispered to himself as Thayn dropped from the tree.

"These are amazing," Thayn noted, eating another berry. Its juice was strong.

Intoxicating.

Thayn bound up the outcrop and gingerly touched its smooth stone wall. "This would be an important place someday."

"You've said that. What kind of place?"

"A great city."

"This?" Leok asked, looking around them.

"This woods would grow out and away from this rock. Around it the Center would be built." Thayn ate another berry. He remembered sharing berries of different colors with Ava and Rykos, applying incantations of Kala to rebuild Yutor. "The trees would retreat to form the Ring and a Wooden Wall embracing the city.

"Along here – " he turned as he gestured, dividing a wide arc " – would run the outer paths. The homes of the Genexus and the fields would be between them.

"Here – " he indicated the foreground " – between

the Center and the Great Path would be the school, the market and all that –

" – and this – " Thayn continued, twirling and returning to the rock wall again, touching it " – is the most important part of the Center."

He closed his eyes and whispered. The Doors of Choosing blinked. Thayn made sure that he remembered the words. *"Trea abba acca adda..."* The Third Door cracked open, then shut.

Leok heard his words, amazed.

*

Nicca expected that Leok would return to the Great Clearing with news of Thayn's death. She didn't expect to find Leok with a rope around his neck, a rope held by Thayn. She did her best to hide her confusion.

"You're back," she greeted Thayn, staring at Leok. "I didn't expect you so – "

" – alive?" Thayn asked.

Nicca grabbed Leok by the arm.

"Don't touch him," Thayn hissed, tugging on the rope.

She let go of Leok in alarm.

"He's mine. I found him in a tree." Thayn's voice returned to normal. "You let him go – and I found him."

Nicca thought for a moment. "He's yours, then – " she capitulated " – if you want *really* want him."

Her tone suggested that Leok was unworthy and that Thayn was a fool. She added carefully, "What of the others? Ayan's captains?"

"They're dead," Thayn replied coolly.

Nicca looked hard at Leok but his expression betrayed nothing.

Thayn, Leok and Nicca returned to her shack. It featured a woven ceiling now. Thayn went outside and looked up. His web had been cut from the trees and brought inside with other weavings that adorned the walls. Nicca taught those of the Great Clearing – she called them her "subjects" – Thayn's method and applied it to decorative purposes. They had been busy.

"How nice the place looks," Thayn observed. "Almost like home."

"You may have it back, of course." Nicca gestured to Thayn's web, explaining, "I didn't know how long you'd be gone."

"You were prepared for any possibility, I'm sure. Keep it." Thayn and Leok left the shack.

*

Nicca followed, hoping to have a moment in private with Leok. What, she wondered, had happened to him? "I – " she trailed off, watching Leok climb a tree followed by Thayn.

*

They made their camp nearby, both on the ground and in new webs high overhead. In the days that followed Thayn and Leok spent much of their time scouting for food. They collected vine and saplings, too. Thayn taught Leok how to weave. A network of bridging spread through the trees above the Great Clearing.

Nicca, too, wanted vine for her subjects. Thayn and Leok expanded their searches. They located reserves in the nearby woods.

Thayn remembered all the sources of mushrooms, fruit and grain that he and Leok had discovered. He scratched maps on thin pieces of smooth stone showing their locations, updating them. They transplanted vines and scattered soil into new locations. Thayn taught Leok how to harvest carefully, making sure to balance what they took with the promise of more to come.

Leok discovered different grains and he and Thayn tested them. They developed various breads agreeable to all. "Rykos would be proud of you."

"Rykos?"

"A baker I used to know."

*

Thayn and Leok found a fissure within the woods surrounding the Great Clearing. From deep within it Thayn heard the gurgle of water. He and Leok set to work.

Nicca asked, "What are you doing?" She was suspicious of anything that she hadn't approved in advance.

"Digging."

"You're making a mess," she objected.

"Come back later." Thayn and Leok built a primitive wash station. It was strenuous work, but a necessary part of Thayn's plan. Berries fortified them.

Thayn and Leok provided the Great Clearing with fruit and bread every morning. At first they left whatever they collected outside Nicca's shack. The earliest to arrive took more than their share. After that, Thayn and Leok scattered foodstuffs throughout the woods. Only when everyone had to search was there food enough for all.

Their work kept them busy. By day, together, they foraged. By night Thayn patrolled the treetops. Leok baked. Most of their work was unobserved.

Nicca was happy to take full credit for their labors. When asked about Thayn and Leok, she was evasive. When her subjects thanked her for everything that

Thayn and Leok did, she feigned modesty and replied, "No, *I* thank *you*. You make me who I am." Nicca lavished her subjects with attention. It was a strategic step in her control of them.

Her favor, however, was erratic. Someone whom she overwhelmed one day, she ignored the next. Yesterday's favorite was forgotten tomorrow. Her leadership was a cycle of possession and neglect.

Nicca grew bored. It made her dangerous

*

Thayn sensed Nicca's growing restlessness. He reached out in thought to a nearby clearing and from it brought a few newcomers. Entranced, they assembled outside the woods and waited until Thayn appeared. "There's so much I want you to know, but not now. The time will come." He led them to Nicca's shack and called to her.

She met him at the door. "What is this?"

"I found them sneaking around outside the Great Clearing. Will you instruct them in our ways?"

"Come, friends." Nicca welcomed them into her shack without a word to Thayn.

Thayn smiled. When Nicca grew tired of the newcomers, he would bring her more.

CHAPTER NINE
The vices of Vok

As youngsters when his twin tripped over Vok's foot or got into trouble for something that Vok did, Vok imagined an audience watching him. Faces of different colors smiled at him admiringly. Gray faces smiled at Vok's avarice and red faces smiled at his anger. These creatures, manifestations of his vanity, became Vok's steadfast friends.

When Vok fled through the Fourth Door and fell to the desert, these same creatures accompanied him. To some of the stolen youth of Kala they acted as guides and mentors. Others were frightened by Vok's vices. Laerl, Ayan, Nicca and their new friends found themselves, with the creatures' coaching and coaxing, natural leaders among those who cowered and cried. Leok seemed oblivious to them.

These creatures visited Thayn now.

At present a white creature preoccupied him. To Thayn it possessed simple beauty and brought him unconditional satisfaction. It soothed him, offering relief from the paces through which he put himself. Thayn sat and contemplated it.

"Are you ready?" Leok called to him every morning.

Increasingly, Thayn replied, "No." Leok foraged by himself.

Thayn had been visited by creatures of every color. Most of them he ignored. The influence of the white creature, however, was undeniable.

"Are you going on patrol?" Leok called to him every evening.

"Yes," Thayn lied. He loafed while Leok baked.

The white creature interfered with the plan that Thayn had roughed out for Leok and himself. Thayn didn't seem to notice, which posed a greater problem. No longer was there purpose or progress on his part.

*

Early one morning Leok distributed foodstuffs. He worked alone more and more frequently. Thayn remained in his tree in communion with his new friend. Leok was unaware of the white creature.

"Psst."

Leok heard a familiar whisper, then nothing. He continued on his way.

Then, "Psst," he heard again.

He stopped and turned.

"Are you alone?" Nicca emerged from the morning shadow. "Finally, a chance to speak with you."

There had been many chances. Leok said nothing.

"Your bread has improved."

"Is it sweet enough for you?" Leok asked.

"It could be sweeter."

"It was, but because of it Ayan made an example of me." They continued in clipped conversation punctuated by hesitations as inferences were quickly made.

"Where's Ayan now?"

"I don't know."

"Is he a threat?"

Leok smiled. "I don't think so."

"What of his captains?"

He looked away too quickly.

"Thayn tells me they're dead. You'll tell me the truth, Leok. Are they?"

"Perhaps." He shrugged. "I don't know."

"You can talk to me."

Leok's tone changed. "I can do many things."

"Yes, of course." Nicca realized that her usual

manner with him wasn't working. She he had never considered crying or flirting with Leok. She sobbed, "Why do you serve him?"

Leok looked at her oddly. "What?"

"Why do you serve Thayn now?" She kissed him. "What about me?"

"You?"

"Yes, *me*."

"What do you want me to do?" Leok asked.

"With creatures of what color do you spend your time?" Nicca demanded.

Leok hesitated. He wasn't aware of the creatures.

"Gray?" Nicca asked.

"Yes," Leok guessed. He lied well, adding, "You see them, too?"

"Since Laerl left the creatures hate me, but I don't care. The gray one – that's good."

"Yes, good." Leok was satisfied with their conversation and turned away.

"I'll tell him." Nicca smiled.

Leok stopped short. He turned back again. "Who do you mean – Laerl?" he asked.

"I will rule Laerl, too," Nicca snapped. She carefully pronounced, "Vok."

"You speak to *Vok*?"

"I do."

Leok swallowed hard.

"Yes." Nicca could sense his fear. "You do well to think twice."

Leok regarded her carefully. Nicca's expression divulged nothing. "What do you want me to do?" he asked again.

"Tell me what I want to know."

"What *do* you want to know?"

"Tell me everything."

*

"No, don't. Stop," Laerl pleaded. "Don't stop."

Nestled within the temple of black crystal Laerl continued his lessons. He had lost all track of time. For an eternity, it seemed, he had been gazing into his dais, learning from his master's mind.

A bush grew at his feet. From it Laerl had eaten berries of every combination of colors. The strength of the berries and his imagination, mingled together and misshapen by Vok, transformed him.

Often Laerl witnessed places of great wonder, such as the edge of fear and faith. More often he learned from horrors – visions of abuse and torment that were effective – and strangely addictive.

Frequently he was drawn to the pool that welled in

the middle of the temple floor. Laerl stood tall, no longer a youngster of Yutor who endured the crimes that Vok had committed against his city. A surfeit of violence and honeydrop fed his hunger as he grew ever more powerful.

"Laerl."

He approached the pool. It steamed.

Laerl cast off his rags and stretched. He achieved a definition of perfection that mocked itself. He dove into the pool and was pulled along a tunnel of smooth stone.

"Laerl. Come to me."

Laerl broke the surface of a new pool. A grotto sheltered it. The water boiled but didn't burn him. Slime swelled from the pool and flowed through a contorted archway. Through the opening, as its heir apparent, Laerl beheld the land of Vok.

From behind Laerl the voice called again. He followed it up a narrow tunnel to enter twin domes, the Diversionary of Vok. Jagged gray stone formed its walls. In the center of both domes a ring of fallen pillars surrounded a single standing column.

Laerl sat on a pillar. From a column stepped the likeness of Vok. Laerl was attracted by Vok's repugnance. Again he wore a cloak made from the faces of his victims, Laerl's father among them.

*

When not in the Diversionary or learning at the dais, Laerl sat and stared into space, unthinking, his cheeks running hot and wet with tears. Sometimes, without tears, he wept.

His latest interlude had been horrifying. He was sparring with Vok as usual – forever on the edge of victory and defeat – but this time, as they fought, Vok grew younger and younger.

He and Vok circled each other, smiling. Sparks danced from Laerl's fingertips. Before it was over, Vok was no older than Laerl himself, and handsome. Laerl was repulsed by his adversary's attraction. A raw counterbalance lasted until the session was over.

Laerl returned to the dais. He was drenched with sweat. He sat and pulled his knees to his chest.

Voices came from within the stone. Nicca's, high and clear, asked, "When?"

"Soon," Vok replied.

*

Life in the Great Clearing improved. Nicca's subjects became expert at Thayn's way of weaving and adapted it for a variety of uses, housing, clothing and, most of all, for decoration. Nicca's shack was draped in fine netting both inside and out.

Between trees the stolen youth of Kala stretched their vines and wove busy patterns to fill otherwise idle hours. They wove as much vine as Leok was able to harvest.

Nicca visited among her subjects. "For me?" she pretended to ask, taking whatever she wanted. She selected the best of their weavings.

"I can tell you were thinking of me when you wove this," she added, "it's so beautiful."

By sharing the spotlight with everyone, half of the attention was always on Nicca. None of them realized that the selected weavings, once taken to her shack, were unwoven by her friends and the vine recycled.

To her people their weaving brought pride and purpose. They wove clothes for themselves and took interest in their appearance. Leok expanded the wash station. Dressed in their best, they walked among their handiwork as if in a gallery. A primitive culture developed. Nicca, wearing the finest of their finery, a chain of flowers above her oval eyes, circulated among them like a jealous spider.

*

Thayn spent most of his time in his tree. Two creatures visited him now, the white one that he found so diverting and a black one with which Thayn shared his meals.

Leok performed his chores unaware of the creatures. When he returned with fruit or finished baking bread, Thayn took first pick and returned to his tree. The web in which he reclined hung lower.

He offered Leok no help at all. Thayn saw no inequity in it. None of the others helped, either. Besides, everything was thanks to him – Thayn – wasn't it? Even Leok owed him.

Thayn said these things to the white creature and the black creature. The former yawned in agreement. The latter chewed in consent.

Thayn didn't know that Leok had again befriended Nicca. He didn't know that Nicca spoke to Vok. Or perhaps, in the company of these creatures, he didn't care. Thayn yawned and chewed, too.

His contemplations were interrupted by the appearance of another set of eyes. A third creature visited Thayn, a familiar face, gray and smiling. It sat in the next tree.

The other creatures hissed at it.

This was the creature that Thayn tried to catch when he first arrived – it bit him on the leg instead. It stared at Thayn and smiled.

Thayn grew uncomfortable. He turned away from the creature, shifting his weight. Branches supporting him creaked and swayed.

The creature laughed at him.

"Go away," Thayn told it. "I'm not interested in you anymore."

It shook its head. The leaves around it shook, too, and it was gone. Despite his words, Thayn felt an irresistible urge to follow. He reached to a branch above him, but the black creature placed a loaf of bread in his hand.

Thayn settled back and gnawed on it, looking at the white creature. He always found comfort in its smile. There was nothing more that Thayn needed.

*

The following day Thayn's ruminations were again interrupted by the hissing of his new friends. The gray creature had returned to a nearby tree. He held out his hand and another creature joined it. Thayn remembered its yellow face and a smile of pointed teeth.

The white creature screeched and the black creature threw food at them.

These newcomers' thoughts came to Thayn along with second thoughts and suspicions. "Beware. Her power grows," the yellow creature warned.

"Whose power?" Thayn asked.

"Nicca's."

"That's nonsense," Thayn scoffed.

The white creature agreed. "She's of no consequence."

The yellow creature asked, "Really?"

"Everything below is because of you," added the
gray creature. "You're responsible for all that is glori-
ous."

"Of course," Thayn agreed.

"Yet Nicca takes credit."

"There's no harm in it," the white creature replied.

"No harm?" questioned the gray creature.

"She'll take everything for herself," the yellow
creature predicted.

"No," the black creature disagreed.

"You no longer know what you have to lose."

Thayn had no reply.

Then, "Why are you here?" the gray creature asked
Thayn.

He thought for a moment. "I'm here to – the youth
of Kala – "

The black creature handed him a piece of fruit.

" – thank you." Thayn bit into it. "Delicious."

"The 'youth of Kala,' as you call them, are *here*,"

the gray creature reminded Thayn, gesturing below. "You must rule them."

"I do."

"You do not," the yellow creature contradicted him in a challenging tone.

The gray creature continued, "She sits in her shack draped in fine weavings. Your subjects, blinded to her ways by the very comforts you provide them, sing her praises. Yet she tells everyone all is her doing. It's a lie."

"It's an appearance," Thayn explained.

"Her power grows," the yellow creature repeated.

"She has no power," Thayn insisted.

"Her power doesn't come from you," the gray creature replied.

"Exactly – as I just told you – I've given her no power."

"Her power comes from elsewhere."

"What do you mean?"

"Hoo-oo-o," howled the yellow creature. Thayn remembered that howl.

"That's impossible." Fear seized him. "Vok?"

"It's true."

"What do I do now?"

"Rid yourself of *them*." The gray creature pointed

to those sitting beside Thayn, white and black.

"You have no right," cried the black creature. The white creature hissed.

"But they're my friends," Thayn objected, "and your brothers."

"They work for her. Traitors. They work to seduce you," the gray and yellow creatures accused in an alternating chorus.

Fear yielded to anger. A new creature appeared, a red one. Without another word the white and the black creatures fled.

Thayn wondered, "What's come over me?" He stood up unsteadily. The yellow creature and the red creature supported him.

*

Leok returned that evening from a full slate of chores. He was surprised to find Thayn exercising. Instead of reclining overhead, he used a low branch to chin himself, pausing at Leok's arrival. "Leok."

"Thayn?"

"Good to see you, Leok. I've neglected you lately. How are you? Tell me what's new. How's Nicca?" Thayn placed his fingertips on either side of Leok's head. "Let me offer you some relief from your toils."

Leok flinched at Thayn's touch, no longer used to

the attention. It meant little to him, whether it came from Thayn or Nicca. He smiled at Thayn's attempts to please him, waiting patiently until Thayn felt that he was back in his good graces.

*

Thayn fasted and continued his exercises. Leok wondered at his transformation. As if new powers had come to him, he was quickly himself again.

*

In the temple of black crystal Laerl completed his instruction. He replicated Thayn's exercise in anticipation of their engagement. Laughter crackled from the dais.

"Finally," Vok whispered, "my champions are ready."

CHAPTER TEN
Champions

Leok had complained of Thayn's recent inactivity and lack of fitness to Nicca. She no longer considered him a threat. Instead, Ayan's captains frustrated her. Nicca could get no information about them other than Thayn's lie that they were dead.

It didn't matter, Nicca finally reasoned. Vok heard her prayer. Laerl would soon return.

*

Leok didn't betray Thayn's lie. Nor did he tell Nicca of Thayn's rehabilitation. Leok thought only of himself. He intended to help no one.

*

Thayn reacquainted himself with aspects of the Great Clearing. He was astonished at its transformation. Splendid weavings hung lashed between its slender tree trunks.

He donned finery to rival Nicca, leggings, a cape

and a crown of leaves. He visited her shack.

Thayn was even more astonished at Nicca's transformation. Washed and dressed in the best weaving that the Great Clearing had to offer, she was almost beautiful. She acknowledged him, startled. "Thayn."

"Nicca."

"A surprise – "

" – as always," he concluded.

"Yes."

"Nicca, I owe you a great apology. An apology for my neglect." He gestured widely. "I owe the same to all of the Great Clearing. I've been no better than an inattentive father, thinking provisions were responsibility enough. No. It's more than that. I hope I'm not too late."

She blinked, staring at him. "Too late for what?"

"To offer to you my undivided attention. My constant companionship."

Nicca thought for a moment. "You're too generous. Don't be a hero, not on my account."

"Nicca, why can't I describe you as I'd like? The nouns decline as they should, but the verbs refuse to conjugate, to say nothing of – "

"What do you mean by – ?"

"But," Thayn continued, "I've learned the error of

my ways. I'll no longer neglect those who depend upon me, those who need me – nor you. I'll abandon camp and join you here. I'll deliver to you – *us* – additional subjects. Together we'll continue to compound our greatness until every inhabitant of the land answers to our will and whim."

Thayn didn't leave the shack.

*

The following morning when Thayn awoke, Nicca wasn't there. He tilted his head and listened. She stood outside the door in whispered conversation.

"I owe you nothing," Leok replied.

"You're so inept. He *has* to be killed. Haven't I made this clear? He's grown too powerful. It needs to be a collective effort, yes. We have to work together."

"What's your plan?" came another whisper that Thayn didn't recognize.

"We'll have a reception. Tell everyone to come to me when the sun is high. At my signal they'll approach to honor him, to have but a touch of him – and we'll tear him apart with our bare hands."

*

Nicca didn't return to the shack. At mid-morning Thayn emerged. Nicca sat under a day tent of woven vine.

Thayn joined her.

"Good morning," she greeted him sweetly. "Did my snoring keep you awake?" Her question, he could tell, was meant to be overheard. Thayn found it curious. What picture was she attempting to draw of herself in the minds of others?

"Did mine?" he countered.

Nicca shrugged. Thayn took a place next to her and they sat, sharing nothing but growing tension.

A couple walked nearby admiring the weavings that hung along the edge of the clearing. Thayn called to them. "Denizens, welcome. What are your names?" He invited them forward with a sweep of his hand.

"Veros," the young man offered. He looked out from under a pronounced brow.

"And you?"

"Mya." A blonde braid fell down her back.

"And who am I?" Thayn asked.

They both looked at him blankly.

Nicca broke the awkward silence. "Thayn," she admonished him, coaching Mya at the same time.

"Thayn, yes," Mya repeated.

Thayn scrutinized Nicca, then Mya. With a laugh his tone changed. "Veros, let's talk." Thayn spoke quickly and quietly. "Don't you know I'm responsible for the weaving you wear? Don't you know I'm responsible for all you eat and drink? Don't you know I'm responsible for your safety? I'm responsible for everything."

Veros looked at Nicca. "He isn't who brings food in the morning."

"No. This is Thayn. This is – *he* is – " Nicca considered her words " – everything he *says* he is."

"Indeed," Thayn agreed. He looked at Nicca with a confident expression that disturbed her.

"Here, at this spot," Nicca quickly proclaimed, although only Veros and Mya stood with them, "when the sun is high, all our people will come to honor him – Thayn – I mean *you*," she continued, addressing Thayn now. "I'll tell them then of your gracious decision to have a more – immediate – influence on our humble lives."

"Let my influence begin now." Thayn reached out his hand to Veros and Mya. Two white berries fell from his hand. He told them, "Eat these."

They did. The effect was instantaneous.

"Go."

Veros and Mya ran into the trees, laughing.

"And tell your friends," Thayn called after them. By the throw of the stones and the counting of moons, the Choosings of the stolen youth of Kala were long overdue. Several of them approached the day tent.

Thayn glanced at Nicca. She tried to disguise her distress with a vacant expression. Having yet to guess what chain of events he had set in motion, she knew that Thayn threatened her plans.

He smiled. "Hurry, everyone." Soon Nicca's subjects crowded around him.

*

Nicca retreated to her shack. Her friends joined her, Leok among them. Nicca peered out a window. "What is he doing out there?" she demanded.

The last of her inner circle appeared in the doorway, laughing. One of them wiped berry juice from his chin. The other explained, calling, "Come, it's our time." They both held sprigs of white berries. Nicca finally realized that she was defeated. Thayn offered them something that she couldn't match.

"Yes," she snorted, pushing her way out the doorway. "It's time."

She left the shack.

*

Thayn watched Nicca. She looked overhead and repeated, screaming, "It's time. Now or never. We have an agreement. It's *time*."

Her subjects watched, too.

The clearing shook. Light flashed and, out of thin air, Laerl appeared before her. Holding his fingertips to the side of his head, he whirled around. He seemed, at first, as surprised to see everyone as they were to see him. After taking a deep breath he squared his broad shoulders.

Laerl was dressed the same as Thayn in leggings, a cape and a crown. Nicca took his arm.

Thayn still stood before the tent distributing white berries to a thinning crowd. Most of Nicca's subjects had already retreated into the trees.

Laerl and Nicca joined Thayn.

"Are you ready for your berry, Laerl?" he asked.

"I've had plenty," Laerl replied.

Their eyes locked. Laerl's preparation for the inevitable confrontation was complete. By comparison, Thayn was no less formidable. "We'll see."

"Kill him," hissed Nicca.

"Call your friends," Laerl urged her, rubbing his head. "We'll use them. It'll be more interesting that way."

Nicca whistled for her friends. Leok obeyed, but no one else came out of the shack. None of her subjects appeared.

"Your followers are otherwise occupied," Thayn observed.

Laerl narrowed his eyes. "Then I'll attend to you myself. My powers are fresh. I'm more than your match." He inclined his fingertips. From them he shot a bolt of light toward Thayn.

Thayn did the same. His bolt met Laerl's, consuming it.

"I don't agree with your assessment of our powers." Thayn sprang away and pointed at Laerl. "Your powers may be fresher than mine, even greater than mine – although I doubt it – but I have a feeling you don't know how to use them. You've had no practice.

"I have more ability in my little finger – " from it a bubble of light flew toward Laerl and burst " – than you have in your – whatever it is you have. Oh, and by the way, Nicca prefers me."

Both of them looked at her. "What?" Nicca appeared confused. She took a step backwards.

"Even Vok prefers me," shouted Thayn. The earth shook.

Several small yellow creatures appeared. "Hoo-oo-o." Fear. Then, pushing through them, red creatures came. Anger.

Creatures of other colors joined them. They stood

everywhere, the vices of Vok.

A creature of a new color revealed itself. Pink. It winked at Thayn.

At first its presence soothed Thayn. Then it conveyed to him a measure of emptiness unlike anything that he had ever felt. Only Laerl would appease it.

"Control of the Great Clearing – dominion over all who inhabit it – the land – and all that's at stake – which is everything – " Thayn and Laerl looked hard into each other's eyes " – I'll wrestle you for it."

Nicca laughed. "What kind of foolishness is this? '*Wrestle* you for it?'" she asked.

The pink creature winked at Laerl, too. With an expression that Nicca couldn't comprehend, Laerl regarded Thayn. "I accept."

"At dawn." Thayn took quick strides to the edge of the Great Clearing, leapt up a tall tree and was gone.

CHAPTER ELEVEN
The Abysm

Nicca awoke before dawn and looked across the shack. "Laerl?" Finding herself alone, she hurried out into the Great Clearing. The moonlight was strong.

Again Thayn and Laerl stood staring at each other. They wouldn't begin their confrontation until the first shaft of sunlight reached through the trees, but they were ready.

Their bond was undeniable. White blond, Laerl almost glowed, poised and powerful. Thayn, darker by comparison, seemed sleeker and stronger. Hair fell across his face, but he didn't bother to brush it away.

"Don't begin without me," Nicca called to them. She raised her hand to her lips and whistled a single high note.

Leok appeared.

"Bring the morning goods here," she ordered him.

"We'll offer entertainment with breakfast today."

Leok obeyed. The moon disappeared as the opposite sky grew light. He returned with baskets of fruit and loaves of bread.

Those of the Great Clearing assembled. Most of them yawned and rubbed their faces, having slept little after eating the white berries. They became more attentive as they saw that something out of the ordinary was about to happen.

Neither Thayn nor Laerl moved.

Nicca turned her attention to her subjects. She walked among them, offering foodstuffs. "Breakfast," she called.

With every piece of fruit and loaf of bread that she distributed she whispered, "Listen for my next message. Spread the word."

Soon everyone had arrived. The sun rose. "We're ready," Nicca proclaimed aloud.

Thayn and Laerl studied each other but remained still. They sensed each other's soul.

The crowd whispered, "What's happening? What does Nicca mean?" they asked one another.

Their whispering grew into murmurs, then catcalls to Nicca. "What is this all about?" everyone wanted to know.

As if in response to their questions, Thayn and Laerl slowly circled each other. Laerl thrust forward his foot attempting to trip Thayn. Thayn darted sideways and Laerl missed him. Having calculated for impact, Laerl fell backwards to the ground.

"O-oh," went the crowd.

Laerl scrambled to his feet and they circled each other again.

Nicca took a step forward, smiling, and announced, "It has begun. You know them both. Laerl, Perpetuant of Vok, and Thayn – our 'Protector.' Our future hangs in the balance. They fight for us."

"Hand to hand. Agreed?" Thayn asked Laerl.

"Agreed," Laerl replied, again trying to trip Thayn. Thayn let him make contact, jerking his leg up as he fell and bringing Laerl down with him. Together they jumped up and backed away.

Again they circled each other. Laerl faked a lunge. Thayn dodged it but Laerl leapt sideways, catching Thayn by the ankle and pulling him down. Thayn fell and Laerl sprang on top of him.

While Thayn and Laerl fought, Nicca circulated among her subjects and whispered, "At my signal, kill them both. Do whatever it takes. Show no mercy." Nicca wanted everything for herself.

Then loudly she added, "I'm so glad you could come."

Nicca failed to appreciate the quality of Thayn's hearing. Nor did she comprehend his ability to know her mind. Her banter didn't last long.

Thayn rolled over Laerl and scrambled to his feet. He reached out in thought, not to Nicca, but past her. Everything was ready now. He whistled three notes, the second higher than the others.

He tried to share his thoughts with Laerl, but his opponent's mind was inaccessible to him. They sprang at each other again.

As they fell to the ground Thayn whispered to him, "Nicca intends to betray you. She plans on killing us both."

Laerl scrambled away. "I don't believe you." He inclined his fingertips and aimed them at Thayn.

"Now," Nicca commanded.

"No," Thayn warned everyone, but Nicca's subjects attacked him. At the same time streaks of light leapt from Laerl's fingertips.

Nicca's subjects attacked Laerl, too.

Streaks of light struck both Thayn's attackers and Laerl's attackers. They screamed and fell.

"Now?" Nicca asked as if an echo, looking around,

confused. Through the trees she saw what she least expected.

Invaders. They were led by young men with white blond hair. Ayan's captains, and Ayan.

Fighting broke out among Ayan and Nicca's followers. Thayn disappeared with a blast of light that knocked everyone to the ground.

Allegiances quickly shifted. Leok called to Nicca. "I know a way. Come with me."

"And Laerl." Nicca pulled her own attackers off him and helped Laerl to his feet. They pushed their way out of the Great Clearing and through the trees.

Leok took the lead. "Follow me. Quickly." They left the trees and hurried across the stubble, arriving at the outcrop. Leok described Thayn's incantation that opened the Third Door. They let go of Laerl and he collapsed.

"The incantation – go ahead, recite it," Nicca demanded. "What are you waiting for?"

"There's something I want you to know." Leok cleared his throat and spoke clearly. "I don't like you, Nicca. You're fickle – and charmless."

Nicca's oval eyes grew round. Even if she wished to disguise her reaction, it was too late. She shrieked, "How dare you talk to me that way, you pustule?"

"Trea abba acca adda..." Leok chanted.

"What?" Nicca asked. "What's that?"

"Trea abba acca adda..." The Doors of Choosing blinked in the wall of rock. The Third Door cracked open. Leok stopped and it snapped shut.

"Treab – caca – What was that you said?"

"Now, let's see, where was I?" After Leok thought aloud to himself he addressed Nicca again. "Oh, yes. As I was saying, I don't like you."

"Yes, *yes*, what do you want?"

"From you?" Leok looked down his broken nose at Nicca. "Absolutely nothing."

"So – "

"That's what I want you to know. This isn't about you, it's about me. Understand?"

She pouted. "Yes."

"Trea abba acca adda..." Leok resumed his chant. The Third Door cracked open again.

"Trea baab caac daad..." replied another voice.

"Who's that?" Nicca asked. The Third Door hesitated.

"Trea abba acca adda..." Leok repeated.

In response, *"Trea baab caac daad..."* the other voice chanted. The Third Door opened by inches and closed again.

140

It was Thayn's voice. He stepped from behind one side of the wall, reversing the spell.

"*Trea abba acca adda…*" Leok continued.

"*Trea baab caac daad…*" Thayn replied.

Leok and Thayn chanted simultaneously and, alternately, the Third Door opened and closed.

The land shook. "Listen – " Nicca convulsed as her body grew fluid and stretched into a familiar, distorted shape.

She stood now as Vok. Her voice was low and raspy. "Listen to me, nephew."

"*Trea abba –* "

"*Trea baab –* "

Thayn and Leok stopped chanting. Laerl revived with the coming of Vok. He looked around at the others, blinking.

"How good to see you, nephew," Vok continued. "How nice of you to journey all this way."

A chorus of laughter replied. Creatures appeared everywhere, white, black, yellow, gray and pink.

Thayn and Laerl walked to each other. Conflicting emotions overwhelmed them. Motionless, they stared at each other.

Vok addressed Leok now. "Fantastic, aren't they? Equal in wisdom, strength and beauty. Their flaw?

They are not *one*. So *all* must belong to *each, alternately*."

Leok looked at him blankly.

"Alak, you weren't very good at school, were you? They're my champions, you see, and for there to be champions there has to be a game, and for there to be a game there have to be players, more than one.

"To have only one player is boring. Every time the same loser. But not *now,* not *here*."

Vok walked to Thayn and Laerl. "One of you, my champions, will always be on the verge of victory. In *perpetuity*. You don't want to leave me now, do you, nephew?"

Vok's body straightened. His expression relaxed and his voice grew warm and clear. "Never again, son. We'll never part." It was Zayn, his father, who smiled at Thayn now. Zayn's face was animated.

It became a blur. Again his voice changed. "I can be anything you want, anyone you want." Arlos, upon whom Thayn had his first crush, spoke to him. He walked to Thayn and embraced him.

Thayn looked into Arlos' eyes. Gray and cool – spellbinding. Thayn lost himself in them until something within them flickered. A familiar image. In Arlos' eyes, Thayn saw a dais.

Jovia appeared within it. Jad was with her. Light escaped the dais. It was Jovia's blessing.

"No." Arlos covered his eyes. Too late.

"Come home," Jad called.

"*Inexeterna*," Thayn whispered.

The spell broke. "No-o-o," cried a blend of voices, Arlos, Zayn and Vok's.

Again as a distorted, fluid shape, Nicca took several steps backwards. She became herself again.

"*Trea baab caac daad...*" Thayn resumed chanting.

Leok shrugged. "*Trea abba acca adda...*" Again the Third Door inched open.

"*Trea baab caac daad...*" Thayn countered, confusing the door.

"*Trea abba acca adda...*" Nicca joined Leok.

Shouts grew in the distance.

Thayn redoubled his efforts, chanting, "*Trea baab caac daad...*" The Third Door shuddered for a moment and shrugged. Confounded, it slowly shut.

"*Trea abba acca adda...*"

"*Trea baab caac daad...*"

The Third Door no longer responded. Instead a trembling underfoot was followed by a growing rumble. "What's that?" Nicca asked.

The land shook violently. With a snapping noise a new crack grew up the wall of rock. It spread overhead and then down the other side, defining a new opening. The Fourth Door revealed itself.

It opened and swung wide. Thayn leapt onto the threshold and stood to the side. Ayan and his captains came through the trees. They led the youth of Kala through the Fourth Door.

"Hurry," the captains shouted and disappeared.

"Come," Thayn called. Nicca and Leok followed. Laerl hesitated. The Fourth Door slowly closed.

*

Thayn stepped into darkness and fell out of the present. The Abysm swelled around him, awash but not wet, like a buoyant breeze. It carried Thayn away.

He held his hands to his forehead. Thayn sensed the youth of Kala all about him, within him, incorporeal, wards of his thought.

One of them, however, was missing. Thayn concentrated. He reached through a receding rectangle.

*

A lone figure remained upon the outcrop. From its smooth stone wall a great hand appeared. Thayn secured Laerl in his grasp and pulled him through the Fourth Door.

*

How long he drifted out of the present is something that Thayn would never know. Everything happened without sequence, without order or chaos. No finite collection of words exists to describe the Abysm. All words do, but only when divided by none. As such, the Abysm is undefined.

Memories washed over Thayn. Most were happy, but some of them were sad and frightening. Others had yet to occur. They existed in both the past and future. Thayn pushed against the present emptiness and it supported him. He floated through it.

He detected an approaching power. It disturbed the equilibrium of the Abysm as if ripples on water, seeking Laerl. Vok pursued him, Thayn realized, even here. He secured the youth of Kala in his thinking.

Thayn sensed himself as part of a greater consciousness that sorted through thoughts of its own. It discovered Thayn among them.

What was this place? Where did these thoughts come from?

In a flash of comprehension, Thayn understood. He felt himself sail through the Abysm as a streak of light. This was a temple – but they were behind the Fourth Door. Whose temple was it?

Thayn flew through its rarefied space. Within the static shell of eternity he created fleeting eddies. A presence beckoned him, a distant sparkle in the dark. Thayn hurried toward it, looking over his shoulder.

Vok followed him as another streak of light. He screamed, "You'll never escape me."

Laerl buried himself deep within Thayn's thinking. Nicca and Leok clung to him. They trembled at the voice of Vok.

Thayn sought out the flickering light. Calm surrounded it. He squinted. Outlined in luminescence – could it really be – ? Thayn was at once both reverent and wary. He trusted nothing, no one, especially with Vok on his heels – but this countenance was special. Thayn was breathless. "Kala?"

"Yes."

"How can you be here? It's to you I'm trying to return."

"We're everywhere. There – " Kala pointed below them " – and here – " he pointed to his head " – and here – " Kala gestured all around them " – in this more perfect place."

"What place?"

"Don't you know?"

Thayn felt as if he were back in school contemplating how "by making many of one, Kala made one of many." Rykos always exaggerated his confusion in regard to such matters as Ava incessantly failed to explain them to him. Nobody noticed that Thayn didn't understand, either.

"Didn't you come through the Archive of Time?"

Thayn, emboldened by his sense of urgency, ignored Kala's question. Instead he asked, "How will I get back to you if you're here? What about the others? We need to hurry – he's following us."

"Who?"

"Vok."

"What you need to know," Kala assured him, "will come to you – "

" – in response to need, I know," Thayn finished impatiently. "*Now* would be nice."

Kala repeated his earlier question. "Didn't you come through the Archive?"

"The what?"

"I see. You're yet to be out of time. In that case, we've unfinished business. Let's go."

"Go where?"

Kala fell.

"Wait." Thayn reached after Kala and the darkness dropped away. Far below, it soaked into the sand.

* Chapter Eleven *

Kala appeared against the desert, his neck broken. He lay askew, a shape that Thayn knew well – the outline of the body of the land.

Vok fell, too. "Come with me," he called to his nephew, reaching out his hands. He returned to the desert with a grunt.

Thayn looked down at both of them with sudden vertigo. He sensed himself high on a pinnacle, unsupported. Both Kala and Vok stretched below him, familiar lands in which Thayn's identities were impossible to commensurate.

He sensed them struggle to possess him. Thayn couldn't keep his balance much longer. Which way would he fall?

"Oh." Thayn slipped.

PART THREE

CHAPTER TWELVE
Reclaimed youth

Leok sprang from the Fourth Door. He took quick steps until he managed to stop himself. The others stood looking around in awe. Here was a new land more wonderful than the last land was terrible. Rolling hills reached everywhere.

Laerl followed, propelled by an invisible force. He smacked into Leok. Both of them fell into a patch of sweet herb.

With a sharp snap the Fourth Door shut. It faded into a wall of smooth rock. Around a new outcrop, before everyone's eyes, a ring of tender saplings pushed up through the earth.

Leok looked at the stolen youth of Kala. What was this? Not only did they look different – Leok *felt* different, experiencing an unexpected sense of relief.

Laerl helped him to his feet. Even Laerl seemed more at ease. He almost smiled. Where, Leok wondered, was Nicca? Would she look the same? He hoped not.

The land of Thayn welcomed its travelers. Brooks meandered to a misty blue river. In the distance, majestic mountains rose.

Thayn's thoughts were benign. Warm breezes ushered in clouds and a gentle rain. Leok felt something close to joy.

"There you are. Come quickly," Nicca called. She led Leok away from the others. "Let's find a place to confine them."

"Confine who?"

"The others. Quick – or it'll be too late. Ayan or one of his – " Nicca stopped. She was looking up into a tall tree. Leok followed her gaze. New fruit swelled before their eyes as it ripened. "Pick some. I'm hungry."

Leok did as Nicca bid him. The tree continued to grow as Leok climbed. The burgeoning land reached wide around him, magnificent and munificent.

Without warning, the ground shook.

An ugly gnarl of knuckles grasped the far foot of the mountains. Tufts of stubble along them twitched and from them rushed a multitude of creatures, yellow and gray, with pointed teeth. Others followed, pink and red.

"No."

"What do you see?"

"Vok has sent his army after us." Leok hurried down the tree and dropped to the ground. He shouted, "This way."

"Fool. What are you doing?"

"In the wind and water, I sense Thayn's intent."

"What?"

"We need to go this way." Leok ran and the others followed him, frightened. Nicca reluctantly brought up the rear.

Leok led them across the grasslands, over hills and up a shoulder of the mountains. The slope was steep and they grew tired. Why did they flee?

Only because Leok told them so. Some lagged behind. In time they caught up with the others who stopped as the desert came into view. "What is that?" they asked one another.

A narrow isthmus reached across an inhospitable stretch of desert to touch the land of Kala. It was a bridge home.

"Come," Leok called. "Thayn wants us to go this

way."

The others turned their back on Leok and gazed out at the new land again. It was so beautiful. But what was that? Below them in the grasslands, brightly colored, the creatures of Vok pursued them.

Again the land shook. From beyond the far mountains a tremendous shape rose into the air. Everyone screamed as a giant hand reached across the sky. It slapped at Vok's army.

"Run," Leok cried. The youth of Kala scrambled past Leok, Nicca leading the way.

*

Thayn's other hand caused similar screams among the Green Folk. His palm hesitated over their heads. They hid. Yodin, the Green One, stood fearless among them. Sensing him, using Yodin as a guidepost, Thayn aimed his fingertip into the center of their clearing.

The youth of Kala dropped from the hand of Thayn and tumbled to the ground. "Oh," Nicca cried, the first to arrive. The rest of them followed and huddled together in fear. Leok was the last to descend.

As soon as they were safe, the giant finger broke away. It receded through the air and disappeared from sight. Nobody, for a moment, moved.

Then Ayan's captains grew brave and ventured

toward the trees. They returned immediately, shrinking away from emerging Green Men.

Tadin, the Old One, joined Yodin and they whispered together. Then Yodin called out directions to the others. They brought baskets of freshly harvested idleflower and set them in strategic spots. Its pungent odor permeated the air.

The youth of Kala grew drowsy. One of them, an inquisitive young man, was fascinated by the bright white blossoms. He crawled to a basket of them before succumbing to their heady scent, surrendering to sweet slumber.

Curious, the rest of the Green Folk dared to examine the sleeping visitors. They fashioned leafy pillows by binding together tender branches with vine, slipping them under heavy heads. The Green Folk faithfully guarded their unexpected guests.

*

Kala responded to Thayn's touch, redirecting his powerful thoughts quickly throughout the land. Great events were set into motion.

*

In Yutor the day was fine. Owan grabbed a robe from the nearest wash station and slipped through the Wooden Wall. He hurried to the Center.

Ava stood in the open doorway. She seemed surprised to see him. "Owan, I was about to call for you."

"Didn't you?"

"No."

"It was Thayn, then."

Ava closed her eyes. More thoughts came to her. "We have to go – "

" – to the clearing of the Green Folk."

"You already know? Before I do?" Ava pouted. "My own stepbrother."

"Thayn's a Woodsward first."

They met Kaden at the Wooden Wall. "An honor to receive you, Ava."

The Ring, nearly recovered from Vok's violence, was in new leaf. "How lovely," Ava exclaimed.

Woodswarder watched from high in the trees as the High Warden escorted the High Minister and Owan to the edge of their domain. "Be quick and safe. Kala is with you," Kaden assured them.

They made their way across the grasslands to the river. Clouds protected the travelers from the sun and no rats interfered with their progress. They avoided Tordawn, arriving downstream of it. A raft was waiting and Blue Men bobbed beside it.

Another raft appeared on the water. "Ava," called

a familiar voice. The delegation from Eator floated by.

"Yara?" Ava waved. Jad and another Woodsward accompanied her.

Other rafts would follow. High Ministers throughout the land had heeded Thayn and Kala's thoughts. Blue Men attended to their safety while on the water. They guided their rafts through rapids and pulled them across still pools. Those from farthest away had traveled rapidly. Jiator was the most distant city and Lyla, its High Minister, appeared ashen and queasy.

At last the delegations reached the lake. Blue Men pulled the rafts to the far shore where Yodin waited for them. Ava could interpret Yodin's thoughts. He suggested that they camp there for the night.

She spoke to the delegations. "This is Yodin, a friend of Thayn, Owan and Jad. Those for whom we come are in his care. Yodin assures us they will sleep safely until we arrive. Tonight he recommends we rest in preparation for our journey tomorrow to the clearing of the Green Folk."

Yodin nodded and disappeared for the night.

The next morning the delegations made their way into the mountains. Patient Woodswarder assisted the High Ministers. Most of them were old and Dira from Aortor had short legs. They followed an unfrequented route that, although an easier climb, was much longer than the usual path up the sheer face of a cliff. Their progress was slow, but resolute.

Soon idleflower bloomed everywhere. The delegation drank a distasteful but heady brew of its antidote. A high ridge defended by pungent white blossoms led to the clearing of the Green Folk. The High Ministers arrived to reclaim the youth of Kala.

The Green Folk hid from the strangers. They stood in the shadow of the trees and looked on with curiosity. Yodin removed the baskets of idleflower and the youth of Kala, sipping brew, regained consciousness. Some of them remembered their High Ministers and held out their hands to them. Others were unresponsive. Too many were no better than animals.

Ava joined Yara. She looked around at their peers. The High Ministers from Dytor, Kotor and Vutor were old friends and they stood together. So did the High Ministers from Ato and Oto, even more closely bound by the proximity of their cities.

Dira and Lyla, the High Ministers of Aortor and Jiator, greeted each other. Dira, small and stout, was robust in personality. Taller and gaunt, Lyla was as remote as distant Jiator. Talking to herself, Beyra, the High Minister of Iotor, hurried by. "What shall we do?

My, my. May Kala be generous in his guidance." The High Minister of Fotor stood among the stolen youth, shaking her head, recognizing her own.

"Where's Zuxa?" Yara asked.

Ava cast a net of thought around the others and retracted it. "Nobody from Evator is here."

"How can that be?"

*

The High Ministers met. They decided on a course of action and set to work. They sorted the young men and women according to city. Then the High Ministers briefed their respective Woodswarder.

In response to need and prompted by prayer, new powers came to them. They reached into the minds of their youth. As if a Hall of Choosing, their thoughts became diagnostic. "He's for the Ring," a Woodsward determined, running his hand over the head of a young man.

"She's of the Genexus," a High Minister determined, analyzing a young woman. "Here's another Genexus. And she's for the Center."

Due to their modest number, Yutor was able to spare only one Woodsward. Owan worked with Ava. He touched the temple of a young man whose white blond hair was streaked with gray. Laerl grimaced.

* Chapter Twelve *

"He's of the Genexus," Owan concluded.

Across the clearing the High Minister from Dytor called for help. "Can anyone feel something here that we can't?" she cried, gesturing to another young man. Other teams failed to sense anything, either.

Ava and Owan were the last to try. Her lips in a bunch, Ava admitted, "No."

"Must we?"

"I'm afraid so."

The High Minister of Dytor and her Woodsward stood several steps apart. With a snapping noise a crack split the air between them. It started overhead and grew down to form a frame.

"Our spell works," Yara whispered to Ava. "See? The Third Door."

It opened.

"No." The young man slid toward it. He had a broken nose and stringy hair. He caught Nicca by her gown as he passed, growling, "Not without you."

Nicca screamed. Ava reached after her, as did the others, but it was too late. Leok and Nicca disappeared through the Third Door.

"Our spell works *too* well."

*

Ava called to the others, "Now our greater effort

begins. Judge well, be honest, and ask if you're in need of advice." The High Ministers reached into the memories of the young men and women from their cities.

None of them had escaped the taint of Vok. There was little need for counsel. Most of them required cleansing to a critical degree. Fearful faces became expressionless as their minds closed.

Grief would continue. The High Ministers would return the youth of Kala to their cities as little more than living shells. Ava walked among them. Some, she sensed, were with child.

Without the wits to check their own behavior, the youth acted at random, some of them unruly. Several who wandered away were returned by the Green Folk. The present situation would quickly become untenable, Ava realized. It was time for another decision and she made it in the form of a proposal.

Again she called together the High Ministers. Ava asked them to allow those whose minds had been closed to join Vok's other victims already in Yutor. Theirs would be a silent generation. With them Yutor would rebuild its population. "It will be a noble sacrifice of which their families may be proud."

The High Ministers agreed. It was the perpetuity

of Kala.

*

At dawn the Woodswarder assembled and, praying to Kala, received new powers. Half of them, led by Owan, would escort the stricken youth to Yutor. The others would accompany their High Ministers home, a handful of less injured youth returning with them.

Ava, with the help of Yodin, thanked Tadin, the Old One, for his hospitality and service. Green Men waited to escort the delegations to the lake. One party was incomplete. Jad was missing.

Yara found him searching the clearing for Thayn. He tried unsuccessfully to disguise his distress. "It's time, then?"

"All our youth are with Owan's party on their way to Yutor. I'll travel with Ava."

"Thank you." Jad wouldn't leave the Green Folk – not now – not yet.

*

A glint of light flew from the temple of Kala with the return of his stolen youth. It streaked across the desert and entered a place that was remarkably similar, the temple of Thayn.

"Oh," Thayn exclaimed at the intrusion.

"Hush," squeaked a voice.

With effort Thayn pulled his hand from the clearing of the Green Folk and brought it to his head. The spirit of Lor bounced excitedly inside it. "Lor, you're here?"

"Quiet, I say. Vok will hear you. He senses me only as the scrap of an old idea. We've studied to learn you must return back the way you came." In thoughts and whispers Lor taught Thayn words to reopen the Fourth Door. Thayn memorized them. Lor concluded, "Most importantly, as you cross the threshold, push. Push hard and leap. I'll guide you."

Thayn prepared himself. Vok must not perceive him. How would he repeat the incantation in a way that Vok wouldn't hear?

In the rustle of leaves and the ripple of water, yes. A breeze visited the mountainsides. Tall trees fluttered and spoke softly. In reply resounded the gurgling and splashing of springs and falls.

The Fourth Door opened, a vague rectangle of light that grew brighter and clearer as Thayn defined it. He aimed for its threshold. Against it, Thayn sprang.

Alak, Vok was vigilant. He reached after Thayn, again grasping his ankle. With a touch of him, Vok learned Lor's words.

Vok deflected his nephew far off course. Thayn

tumbled out into the desert.

*

Thayn awoke to the light of early morning. The sky stretched over him. He found his feet. Where, he wondered, was he?

Around Thayn in every direction reached the desert, motionless. Tilting his head, he listened – but he could hear nothing. On the far horizon Thayn thought that he saw a vague outline, a hint of land.

What else could he do? He brushed the hair off his brow and, with a deep breath, started walking.

CHAPTER THIRTEEN
The Archive of Time

Thayn groaned. He rolled over and sat up. Without thinking, he rubbed his face. Sand that stuck to his hands scratched his cheeks.

The sunlight was white, intense. It slowly faded. Gray below and blue above, the desert stretched all around him until it met the sky. He stood up.

How long had it been? How many days? He was so thirsty. This was no charm of Vok. Or was it?

Thayn kept walking. Again he stumbled and fell. Again the light grew white. He closed his eyes, but it made no difference.

How often had he fallen? How many times? Was he rolling hills and rippling water? Was he a forgotten thought, something incomprehensible even to himself? Had he fallen from the Abysm and out of consciousness? Or had he fallen from grace?

The light grew right and Thayn stood up again. He opened his eyes and looked behind him. A hot breeze blew and his footsteps filled with sand.

The desert shimmered. Ahead in the distance lay a long, low shape. It sprang upright and sailed through the air, balancing first on one hand, then on the other, dancing in silhouette. Was it Arlos tumbling in the marketplace? Thayn thought that he could hear the sand crunch.

The sound reminded him of his stepfather's loom. One hand, *thap*, then the other, *foosh*. Thayn remembered his household busily preparing bristlecloth. Recently he could imagine his family and be among them. No longer. His powers were gone.

Thayn looked across the desert. It was a hallucination, he decided. Nothing more.

The sun grew red as it set. The shape continued to dance. Or was it real? "Kala?"

Thayn reached out to the horizon. He fell headlong down a bank of sand. With a soft groan, he came to rest on his back and lay motionless.

*

The night grew cold over him. Thayn barely slept, fitfully. He thought that he could hear the rustle of leaves in the wind and the ripple of water. Above him, stars twinkled.

Several sparkles of light streaked through the sky and swirled about his head. "Thayn, awake," one of them called.

"You must get up," squeaked the other.

A strong smell, sweet and warm, came to him. Leafcake. Thayn tried to sit up, but he couldn't move. His concentration wavered and the sparkles of light disappeared.

He remembered a rhyme that his mother taught him about the stars. "Twinkling, twinkling..." Thayn didn't finish. His consciousness drained away as the sky filled with clouds.

*

Thayn continued walking. Or was it all a dream? He groaned. It was cold and he was thirsty. He felt himself drifting again.

He scrutinized the horizon. Without warning the desert opened under him. Thayn was pinned against a slant of sand that spiraled around an empty center and sucked him down. A whirlpool.

Thayn fell through the ceiling of a great chamber and dropped to the floor. Dim, supported by pillars of sparkling sand, the chamber extended without end in all directions. Luminous mist pooled here and there, drifting with an occasional breeze.

Thayn scrambled to his feet, bumping into a pillar. It spilled into a heap of sand at his feet. "Oh-h."

Thayn backed away from it and touched another pillar. It fell, too, emitting a plaintive cry.

The air grew chill.

A streak of light bounced about the chamber and struck not far from Thayn. A pillar grew bright and wispy. It coughed for a moment and wheezed. An old man stood before him.

"Lor," Thayn exclaimed.

"Don't touch me." Lor's voice was shrill. "Don't touch the pillars. They're fragile."

"What are? Lor, what *is* this place?" Thayn asked, looking around curiously.

"This is the Archive of Time," Lor explained. "It is supported by the Dead and the Living."

"By the dead and living what?"

"Not by what – by *whom*." Lor shook his head. "These are the life forces of all who were, are, and are yet to be in all the lands."

"I don't understand."

Lor sighed. "I know. That's why I'm here."

Thayn's frown turned into a smile. "It's good to see you." Thayn took a step toward the old man.

"Don't move. You've done enough damage already." Lor examined the pillars that Thayn had disturbed, two piles of sand on the chamber floor.

"What do you mean?"

"I said this is the Archive of Time. It's supported by all who exist in the past, present and future. Except these two." Lor gestured at the former pillars. "Unless you intercede on their behalf."

"Who are they?"

"That one is of the Dead. He's known to you. Arlos."

"Arlos?"

"You must absolve yourself of his passing." Lor turned his attention to the other pile. "This one is of the Living. He will be harder for you to defend."

"Why? Who is he?" Thayn asked, sure that nothing would match the tender wound that Lor's news already provoked.

Lor regarded the heap of sand. "He's you."

*

The light brightened within the Archive of Time. Thayn heard a growing murmur. As he looked around, the surrounding pillars took new shape. They grew defined, some of them recognizable. The pillars looked from Thayn to the two piles of sand and back again, whispering among themselves.

One of the pillars produced the same silhouette that danced in the desert. His familiar outline first came to Thayn years ago as Forbidden Knowledge. Of greater substance here than in the Abysm was his very being, the warmth and gladness of Kala.

"We meet again, although when I suggested earlier that we're in many places at once, this wasn't what I had in mind." Kala laughed sadly, looking down at the piles of sand. "You're in a heap of trouble."

Two nearby pillars became most prominent. They turned slightly toward each other, broad across, but slim and narrowly featured. They regarded Thayn with cool, gray eyes. Arlos' mother and father. "Again you've taken our son from us," Arlos' father cried.

"Beware the wind," Kala advised Thayn. "If the sand is scattered, his essence, and yours, will disintegrate. It would be as if you never – *were*."

Arlos' mother sobbed.

Lor addressed Kala. "I'm an old spirit. I know well your ways and the ways of Thayn. But of this one, Arlos, I remember nothing. Why?"

Kala replied, "He's guilty of innocence, embraced by contradiction, a victim of love."

"Love?" Arlos' father laughed incredulously. "I

don't believe you."

"Of that, then, we must be convinced. So let the hearing begin." Kala's even voice echoed throughout the chamber. "You, the pillars of our present, past and future, will be our jury. Thayn, Woodsward of Eator, stands before you. On trial is his existence."

Light swirled throughout the Archive. The pillars of Arlos' parents changed in appearance, growing much younger. Their gray eyes blinked. They looked about with curiosity.

A new pillar appeared. It was as if Thayn's had been reconstituted. He was sure that he looked at himself. Then it happened again. They were two pillars now, almost identical, his father and uncle, Zayn and Vok, as boys.

The Archive dissolved and reorganized into a long, tall room of angles and arches, the commons room of the school in Eator. Other children appeared. Arlos' mother, a thin little girl, sat at a table with friends. As the twins walked by them, Vok reached past Zayn to pull her hair. "Ouch," she cried, looking up.

Arlos' father, a skinny boy, came to the table. "What happened?"

"He pulled my hair."

"Zayn," Vok remonstrated. "What's come over

you?"

"I didn't – " Arlos' father grabbed Zayn by the tunic. Zayn pushed him to the floor and Vok laughed.

A woman in a green gown intervened. "What's this commotion?" Elyda demanded.

"Zayn did it," Arlos' mother accused.

"No, I didn't."

"He pushed me," Arlos father added.

"I saw him push you," Elyda agreed. "Zayn, come along with me to the office. I'll write a note to your parents."

"Alak," Vok exclaimed, pretending to hide his delight. As soon as they got home from school Vok announced, "Zayn has a note."

"Zayn, how could you?" scolded their mother as she read it. "I'm so disappointed."

"I didn't – Vok – "

Vok glared a warning at him. Their mother promised, "You'll be punished. To your room, now." That night, when Vok joined him, came the greater punishment.

Again light swirled throughout the Archive. The children grew to maturity. Zayn and Vok, Arlos' parents and others for whom the stones had been thrown joined the High Minister in the Hall of Choosing and their ceremonies began.

For most the First Door opened and returned participants to life among the Genexus. The Second Door led young women to the Ministration and young men to the Woodswarder.

The Third Door expunged from the cities those for whom the other doors didn't open – those who didn't love. They became Outcasts.

Arlos' parents passed through the First Door.

For Zayn the Second Door opened. Vok, whose turn was next, attempted to join him.

Zayn could endure him no longer. Jovia, the High Minister, interceded on Zayn's behalf. He ran to the First Door and slipped through it. Vok attempted to stop him. He raised his arm to Jovia. The Third Door swung wide and, through it, backwards and by his heels, Vok disappeared.

The room swirled and the pillars shifted. Life among the Genexus resumed. Unexpectedly, Zayn married Kalia, a pretty young woman who herself recently returned through the First Door. Arlos' parents wed, too. Arlos and Thayn were born. Their likeness reached up in vapor over respective spills of sand.

Years went by. Arlos and Thayn grew from infants into sprightly boys. Although they knew each other, they grew up in different parts of the city and were schooled in separate classrooms. They never became close friends.

Changes in Zayn's behavior occurred. Sometimes he lapsed deep into thought, whispering to himself. He often left at night for hours at a time. Increasingly, he and Kalia argued. Zayn grew abusive and Thayn hated him for it.

Early one morning Thayn heard thumps and thuds. He crept into the shadow of a doorway to the main room of their household. His father sat at the table at which the family took their meals. In front of him sat a stack of old and tattered books.

Monitors and Jovia entered through the front door without knocking. Immediately Zayn became agitated. After heated words Jovia offered, "Return the books to me and I'll only cleanse your thoughts of them."

"Don't touch my mind," Zayn cried. He raised his hand to Jovia.

Something happened that Thayn didn't see. His father slumped over.

Jovia stared at Zayn. She tried to rouse him but there was no response. "I didn't do this," she told the Monitors. They took the books and left.

Kalia found her husband the next morning sitting

at the table staring into space. Zayn was never again himself, his mind closed. Thayn seldom spoke of it.

That morning Arlos looked different to Thayn.

During the following years Kalia remarried twice. Others came to live with them, the new wives of her previous husbands and their children. Ava was the daughter of Daloth, Thayn's second stepfather. Previously schoolmates, now stepsiblings, Thayn and Ava and another friend, Rykos, were already inseparable.

The pillars dissolved and reformed. The young grew older.

It was Thayn, now, who slipped away at night for hours at a time. He didn't know what he did, or why. He didn't know that he, as his father before him, was an agent of Vok. From beyond the Ring of Eator his uncle repeatedly manipulated Thayn's will, borrowing the use of his ears and eyes.

Thayn studied in the library and slipped into the Center. From unsuspecting sources Vok, through his nephew, learned many things.

Over the years Thayn grew more daring. He didn't understand his danger. His thoughts were increasingly of Arlos. Thayn and Arlos both practiced tumbling for their respective nexus.

A young man now, Arlos was broad across, but

thin, with hair uneven shades of brown and cool gray eyes that looked right through Thayn. He was so handsome and talented, Thayn's heart raced at the thought of Arlos and he stuttered in proximity to him.

Arlos didn't notice.

Thayn's trespasses within the city continued and he was nearly caught. Then Vok attacked neighboring Yutor. Its last surviving Woodsward, Kaden, brought Eator the news.

The room continued to swirl.

Through a hedge of grass Thayn watched Kaden race to the Center, his eyes darting and his nostrils flaring. He had never seen a Woodsward up close.

Kaden reported to the High Council. Eator was placed on alert.

Choosings, meanwhile, were long overdue. At last the ceremonies were held. The First Door opened for Arlos and Rykos. For Ava and Thayn the Second Door led them, respectively, to the Center and the Ring. Thayn was a Woodsward now.

The pillars in the Archive appeared as the trunks of trees. Greenery reached overhead. As Thayn made his way through the Ring, Vok called to him. "Come," he implored, appearing to Thayn as Arlos, attempting to lead him into the grasslands.

More than once Thayn resisted Vok's deception. On a visit to the High Chamber, Thayn learned of Arlos' sudden illness and later came word of his death. It was Thayn's punishment.

Arlos' mother swooned, overwhelmed by the succession of events. Thayn reached out to comfort her.

"Don't touch her," Lor scolded. The trial was suspended.

CHAPTER FOURTEEN
Jad's fidelity

The light of another morning broke through the treetops. Jad stretched, stood up and stared out into the desert. He watched for Thayn from an outpost near the clearing of the Green Folk. Once before he, Thayn and Owan traveled to this very place. From there Owan detected, for the first time, the land of Vok.

Jad saw nothing but sand. He climbed down, wondering how long since the delegations of High Ministers and Woodswarder left. Jad was lonely.

Yodin was waiting for him. He smiled sadly. Yodin's yellow eyes were two identical moons in a leafy sky. Of all the Green Folk, it was only Yodin whom Thayn had sensed. He heard Yodin's thoughts and, through their communication, they had become friends.

Jad couldn't hear Yodin's thoughts. Instead, it was Yodin who understood Jad, not his thoughts but his expressions, the tilt of Jad's head and the focus of his gaze. Yodin interpreted him. This young man was incomplete, not in the same way as the recent visitors whose minds were damaged, but in the absence of fulfillment.

Yodin felt a sudden surge of excitement as Jad's heart swelled. A distant tree shook, then another. A figure dropped to the ground.

"Thayn?" Only a whisper escaped Jad's lips. He took a sharp breath. Did the figure wave a hand? Jad took a few halting steps. Then, both laughing and crying, he and Yodin ran to meet him. In a patch of moss, on the brink of consciousness, lay – "Thayn?"

Thayn quickly brought a hand to his brow. He hesitated, pushing at his hair. "Yes," he managed.

"I knew you'd come back." Jad brought a hand to his own brow, too, feeling another overwhelming surge of emotion. "What's come over me?"

Yodin attended to Thayn. After a draught of idle-flower brew he was on his feet again. Jad embraced him, completing a gesture of expectation that he first offered Thayn at the edge of the Well of Understanding. Thayn pulled away.

"Are you hurt? Is it your shoulder?"

"No." Squaring his shoulders, Thayn replied, "I'm

fine – just tired."

"Where were you? How did you get here? The others – "

"They're safe?" Thayn interrupted.

"Yes."

"Where are they now?"

"The High Ministers came – as you requested."

Thayn nodded. "That's good."

"They returned on a finger of land, a great hand, according to Yodin."

Thayn nodded at the Green One. "Yodin, yes."

"When you weren't with them – Thayn, I've been so worried."

"I leapt after them, yes, but I – tripped. Vok tripped me. It was my hand Yodin saw. Then Vok flung me out into the desert. I had to walk."

"From that far away?"

Thayn smiled. "From farther than that."

A reception for Thayn was spontaneously organized. Yodin escorted the Woodswarder to Tadin. The Old One scratched a brown spot on his bushy head. He seemed confused, at first offering his attention to Jad.

Yodin redirected him. Tadin spoke unintelligible words. Yodin repeated them in thought, knowing that Thayn would hear his thinking.

They proceeded to a spring of warm water and the reception began. Green Men brought hearty draughts of idleflower brew. Steam rose everywhere. Relaxed, Jad with his head on Thayn's shoulder, they watched supple acrobats climb together, take on the appearance of young trees, then splinter and sail through the air to assemble again.

The brew, an acquired taste, was potent and soothing. Thayn and Jad watched with eyes half-closed.

Yodin attended to them. Thayn offered him little consideration, regarding Yodin no differently than the others. Nor could Yodin interpret Jad's expressions easily anymore. "Have I done something to offend them?" Yodin wondered.

"Tell me everything that's happened since I left," Thayn prompted Jad.

"Or," Yodin thought, "is the brew too strong?"

Thayn didn't finish it. Instead, he listened attentively to Jad.

Jad related his recent adventures. He described his return to Eator from the Diversionary and lonely time at home. Then he was summoned to accompany Yara here, "as you know." He told Thayn of the damage to the stolen youth of Kala and Ava's offer to provide the youth a home in Yutor.

"Their minds have been closed?" Thayn asked.

Jad nodded. "Most of them."

Thayn smiled sadly. "And so I've failed," he whispered in an odd tone.

"No. You're their salvation – from Vok."

The wind grew suddenly strong and howled in the trees. "Hoo-oo-o."

"Let's not speak his name."

*

The next morning Thayn awoke in Jad's arms. They lay on a slab of mossy rock to one side of the spring. Green Men, Yodin among them, waited upon their pleasure. Thayn and Jad were soon refreshed and ready to begin their journey home.

They returned to the edge of the clearing for a last audience with Tadin. The Old One had trouble attending and, after mumbling several senseless phrases, nodded back to sleep.

Thayn and Jad drank another draught of potion to guard against the idleflower's toxicity, then climbed into the trees. A party of several Green Men joined them. The morning was splendid. Broad leaves allowed sunlight to sift through the understory. Here the idleflower was well-manicured, protecting the clearing of the Green Folk. Woods grew thick as they climbed a ridge, then thinned as the rock fell away in steps.

Jad was at his best in Thayn's company. He noticed wonders everywhere and stopped to share them. From stumps grew spotted mushrooms and brightly mottled moss. Lingering here and there, they often lost sight of their escorts.

A spring seeped from a broad slant of broken stone and grew slick with slime. Thayn slipped and slid, feet first, reaching his arms out above him. "A-o-ah."

"O-a-oh." Jad slipped after him down the hillside, managing only for a moment to stay upright, crouching and extending his arms. Thayn looked up at Jad as they fell, their eyes wide.

Thayn landed with a thump against moldering logs and sprang to his feet. Jad was upon him immediately, sliding headfirst. He brought Thayn down again.

"Oh," Jad laughed.

Thayn almost looked angry. Then he laughed, too.

They both stood and shook themselves off. Their escorts appeared, yellow eyes bright with amusement, and surrounded them.

"Your powers," Jad asked as they walked. "How long have you been without them?"

"What?"

"They're gone, aren't they?"

"Yes," Thayn admitted.

"Then evil is far away."

*

They arrived at the edge of a sheer cliff. Several of the Green Men descended in advance while others climbed alongside the Woodswarder, pointing to handholds and footholds. Thayn and Jad proceeded carefully, descending in a zigzag.

After they reached the base of the cliff only a single scout was required. Jad and Thayn nodded thanks to the remaining Green Men who, after an awkward moment, withdrew. Where was Yodin?

Woods of a different tree grew on the lower slopes. The scout and the Woodswarder continued on their way. They made good progress down the remaining mountainside. The sun climbed high and then began its own descent. A shimmer of light reached through the trees, reflected in water. Jad pointed. "Look."

Thayn glanced up. He paid more attention to his footing since their tumble down the slimy stone. "Yes, good." The shimmer came from the lake.

Jad gazed back up into the mountains. "I regret leaving this place." The thinning woods ended upon a grassy hill that dropped to meet the shore. Carefully they descended a final slope.

Their escort disappeared and Thayn and Jad were greeted by a salutation from the lake. From opposite directions two Blue Men sprang, one overarching the other. They disappeared back into the water.

Jad extended his hand and Thayn grasped it. They waded into the lake. The Blue Men pulled them down into the water. Weedy hair floated around their faces and bubbles escaped their smiles. Securely attached, the Woodswarder rode the Blue Men across the lake, skimming the surface for air.

A great city was nestled in its depths. On previous crossings the Blue Men swam wide around their city. On this occasion they dove toward home. They sensed no haste on the part of the Woodswarder, and news of Thayn's recent deeds had already spread throughout the land. They would pay tribute to him.

The underwater city rose within a living reef, delicate but strong. The Blue Folk skillfully cultivated it, shaping cells with domed ceilings and arched walls. Most of them were small and simple. The greatest of them was half the size of the city. The domes bubbled. Stems of bladderweed reached down from the surface and filled them with air.

Successively smaller cells rose on top of one another and side by side to form complex communities.

Colorful vegetation clung to the walls. Here the Blue Folk lived and breathed. Larger public cells provided opportunities for congregation and free access among the greater population.

The tallest towers of the city belonged to its defenders. Thayn and Jad presently rode members of its fraternity. Many of them watched from within their cells, guarding the waterways. Eels at their side assisted with duty.

The Blue Men spiraled to the lowest dome. It was colossal, oval in shape and crowned high at the ceiling. The Deep, as it was called, was supported by elaborate cells along its circumference. Air from the hollow bladderweed confined a pool of still water. In the most ornate cell floated the High Dyad of the Blue Folk. Lithe and lean, they were barely distinguishable from each other, their faces surrounded by silky blue hair.

The Blue Men somersaulted. Thayn and Jad slipped onto a smooth shelf, breathing deeply, steadying themselves against the stony shell. They looked across the pool. An audience of Blue Folk filled the smaller cells, bobbing in the water, waiting. Jad looked up into the dome in wonder. A translucent ceiling played with trapped rays of sunlight.

A mass of hair and twigs floated to the surface at

the Woodswarder's feet. From under it emerged a large head. A body, plump but frail, followed. With effort, grunting, it pulled itself out of the water and crawled onto the neighboring ledge. An old man or woman, it was impossible to tell.

"Hello," Jad acknowledged.

The old face blinked at Jad and broke into a smile. "Do I believe my eyes? When did you arrive?"

"Just now."

"How is this possible?" After an exchange of gibberish with several passing Blue Folk, and with a great deal of effort, the old figure rose and bowed. "It's a privilege to meet you. We're here to honor you."

"Who are you?" Jad asked.

"The Blue Folk call me Wablub." He sat with a plop.

"From what city are you?"

"I was found long ago in the river. I was a baby boy. That's what they tell me."

"You speak well."

"I've learned from those who cross the river."

"Outcasts? They're not – " Jad worried that he might offend their new acquaintance and finished by saying " – their ways aren't ours."

"Nor are they mine. Nor are mine yours." Wablub

smiled as if to suggest that it was *Jad* who didn't understand *him*.

He continued. "My ways are my own and those of
the Blue Folk. They hold you in high esteem. A rare
honor, and one that shouldn't be accepted lightly. I've
seldom seen others such as ourselves here, and never in
places of distinction. See, the tribute begins."

A group of Blue Folk sprang up out of the water
and arched high into the air. As they returned to the
surface of the water a second group, all men, sprang
from it and, as they dove into the water a third group,
all women, sailed into the air. The three groups retired
to separate portions of the pool to perform simultaneously above and below the water.

The High Dyad joined them. Pairs of Blue Folk
propelled them into the air. The High Dyad tucked
and, after tumbling, unfolded themselves and returned
to the pool without a splash. They withdrew.

The first group concluded their portion of the tribute and retired from the pool. The third group left, too.
Only Blue Men remained, gesturing to Thayn and Jad.
"They want you to join them in the water," Wablub
explained. Again he struggled to his feet. "It's been a
pleasure meeting you."

Thayn and Jad took deep breaths and slipped into

the pool. Two Blue Men transported them to the tallest towers and a cluster of small cells. The domes provided small pockets of air. Between breaths Thayn and Jad lowered themselves in the water to observe the activity occurring all around them. Blue Men participated in some kind of sport, Jad surmised. Newcomers tagged team members who returned to their cells for air. Eels took part in a merry chase.

Jad knew about the Blue Men only from riding them up and down the river. There was so much more to learn. Airy stalks floated on the water, bobbing overhead as they watched the entertainment. Jad realized that the stalk was food. When he and Thayn surfaced to take a breath, they nibbled at it. Delicious.

After the chase concluded, Thayn and Jad climbed onto a ledge that connected the cluster of cells. It offered a poor view of the city but plenty of room. Dry bladderweed was piled along it, soft and spongy, and the Woodswarder gladly crawled into it. "I'm tired," Thayn mumbled. He closed his eyes, snoring.

Stars seemed to shine below them. The colorful vegetation that grew from the lower walls glowed, points of light that soaked through the water. Watching them, Jad, too, fell asleep.

*

Splashing and gibberish came with the dawn. A chorus of Blue Men bobbed in the cells surrounding the ledge. Sunlight reached down from the surface and the lights that Jad had seen below in the dark were gone.

"Thayn," Jad whispered.

Thayn shook himself, seeming to remember many things at once. "Good morning," he replied.

"I think it's time to go."

Thayn and Jad slipped into the water and two Blue Men secured them in place. The waterways were lined with Blue Folk who wished the Woodswarder well. Their hosts swam to the surface of the lake, skimming the water gently, and headed toward the river.

*

It was difficult to ride on the backs of the Blue Men and keep track of anything else. Always the bubbles and the clouds, the whirling blue of the water and the sky, disoriented the Woodswarder and they remembered little but the rush of motion and a gasping for breath.

*

After a morning swimming upstream, Thayn and Jad returned to their senses after somersaulting from their hosts and skidding onto a grassy shore. Across the river Jad saw what he feared. The Blue Men, evidently, didn't appreciate that he and Thayn were without the powers that made Outcasts flee at the sight of them. They had been delivered to the ford at Tordawn. Outcasts on the island called to others already on rafts. They pulled themselves across the river in pursuit of the Woodswarder.

Jad needn't have worried. The rafts rose into the air without warning. Outcasts tumbled into the water as Blue Men disappeared under them.

Thayn and Jad scrambled to their feet.

The Outcasts couldn't swim and were carried away with the current. Those on the shore watched them splash and flail. Thayn and Jad easily escaped.

A path from earlier journeys between Eator and Yutor was still depressed into the grass and they followed it. A few bold rats attacked them. Thayn and Jad tore them from their legs and hurled them away. The Woodswarder quickened their pace.

*

At last familiar woods grew near. Thayn hesitated. "Go ahead without me. Tell Cyrll I need to see him. I'll wait here."

"What?"

"I'm tired." Thayn sat down. "I need a quiet place

to rest."

"We're almost – "

"So tired." Thayn reclined, pulling the tall grass around him.

"What's wrong?"

"Do as I ask," Thayn requested impatiently.

"But – "

Thayn closed his eyes and whispered something. Then, aloud, he said, "Go."

Jad brought a hand to his brow. "All right." He ran toward the trees.

CHAPTER FIFTEEN
Return to routine

Three Woodswarder emerged from the Ring. Jad led the way only for a moment, accompanied by both Tylos and Cyrll himself. Tylos' braids bounced about his shoulders as he and Jad hurried to keep pace with the High Warden's stride.

Thayn stood up unsteadily to meet them.

"You're in need of rest," Cyrll determined immediately. "You're not yourself. I can sense it."

Jad looked at Cyrll, confused. He felt oddly negligent. What had happened to Thayn?

"Yes," Thayn agreed.

Cyrll reminded Jad, "When Thayn returned from the liberation of Yutor he was in much the same condition. It comes as Kala's powers depart."

"He seemed fine until now."

"And because he's home."

"No ceremonies, please," Thayn whispered, "just a place to rest."

"Up in the treetops?" Thayn had convalesced in a crook of branches after he returned from Yutor.

"No – just a bower near the Wooden Wall." Thayn brushed at his skin. "I wish to be clean. To sleep. To be alone."

Cyrll and Tylos exchanged an uneasy glance that included Jad and returned to Thayn again.

"Jad will take care of me," Thayn added hastily.

Jad explained that he had earlier abandoned the bower that Thayn and he once shared.

Tylos offered, "I know of a suitable place. Come." Smiling, he and Cyrll walked on either side of Thayn, followed by Jad.

The vault of the Ring opened high and wide. Fluttering leaves rustled, soft shades of green edged with golden light. Without words Cyrll communicated his intent to the Woodswarder around them and none interrupted their passage.

Tylos led them toward the Wooden Wall. Not far from his tower grew a tight stand of trees. He located within it a modest hollow with a leafy floor around which to build a new bower.

Thayn dropped to his knees and burrowed himself

into the soft mulch. Cyrll nodded and left them.

"Are you hungry?" Tylos asked.

"You've troubled yourself enough," Thayn replied. "Jad will fetch us all we need. Thank you."

"Take care, then." Tylos withdrew.

"Thayn, what's come over you?"

He closed his eyes and whispered.

Jad brought a hand to his brow. "Thayn?"

Thayn closed his eyes tighter.

As if in response, Jad, too, was overcome by exhaustion. Yawning, he reclined next to Thayn and fell into a heavy slumber.

*

Thayn shook Jad. "Wake up."

"Is it morning already? I'm so sleepy," Jad complained. He rubbed his eyes.

"No. It's my powers. They've come back."

"What?"

"And they're strong."

"In response to what?" Jad sat up. "What else do you feel?"

"Nothing."

"Then why have they come back?"

"I don't know." Thayn tilted his head and concentrated. "Perhaps you can tell." He held a fingertip to

193

the side of Jad's head.

Jad's expression slackened for a moment and he stared into space. Then, with a flinch, he returned to himself. "Yes, they're strong. No, I don't sense their reason, either. They feel – different – than last time."

"Does that matter?" Thayn asked quickly.

"I guess not."

He almost closed his eyes. "Wait."

"What is it?" Jad asked.

"Someone is calling me."

"Yara?"

"Yes – no – I don't think so. Someone – some-*thing* – I don't trust it."

"What?"

Thayn shook his head. "I'll ignore it." They sat for a moment in silence. Thayn closed his eyes and, looking away, whispered again.

Jad's eyes opened wide. "I can feel it, too." He scrambled to his feet.

"It's coming from the city."

"Let's go."

On previous occasions, Jad knew, Thayn had been contacted in thought by someone, or something, in the city. Before her passing, Jovia called him to the Forbidden Room to share with him words of power. Later

Yara summoned Thayn to the Center to assist her in a summit of High Ministers. Most recently both Thayn and Jad responded to a powerful pulsation emanating from the Fourth Door.

They hurried to the nearest sector gate. Its guards were unconscious. "What happened?" Jad asked.

"They'll be fine." Thayn opened the gate. "Let's hurry."

"Wait – put on a robe." Thayn complied and they ran down the outer path. The night was still and inky black. The Ring confined its own inner glow, but here, under a new moon, there was scant light.

They entered the Great Path. Several Monitors approached. Thayn and Jad pressed themselves against a wall, hiding in the shadow, unseen. "I'm surprised you didn't hear them," Jad whispered after they were gone. Thayn was known to have keen ears.

"I was listening to the voice."

"What voice?"

Thayn concentrated and told Jad to do the same. "Don't you hear it?"

Jad exclaimed, "It's coming from the library."

"Yes." They made quick progress along the Great Path, remaining close to the wall. Thayn opened a door to the library and they slipped inside. A few large rooms comprised most of the building. Several smaller rooms were nestled in the back.

To the last of them Thayn and Jad made their way. It was unremarkable. Tables provided a quiet place to read. "This way." Thayn lit an oilstem.

He entered an alcove and pressed his palm to the wall. The stone groaned and a hallway appeared. He opened the next wall and a musty smell overwhelmed them. They stepped into a cramped annex laden with thick, worn books.

"The Forbidden Room?" Jad asked, astonished, as the wall closed behind them.

"Hush," Thayn whispered. He pulled an old tome from the corner of the highest shelf and, page by page, examined it.

He replaced the first book and retrieved a second one. "Thayn?" He ignored Jad who finally sat on the floor and leafed through a few books himself.

*

"Thayn, it's – "

"What?" Thayn replied impatiently.

" – it's nearly morning."

"Already?" He closed the book that he was examining, returned it to its place and opened the wall. "We have to go. Hurry."

They retraced their steps to the Wooden Wall. The sector gate was closed. Faint noises followed them up the outer path.

Again Thayn and Jad sought out the shadows, hiding as Genexus delivered carts laden with foodstuffs. After they left, dazed guards emerged to retrieve the carts. Thayn and Jad slipped through the gate.

They rested all morning and into the afternoon. An unobtrusive steward checked on them and reported to Cyrll that they slept.

Again, after dark, Thayn and Jad returned to the Forbidden Room. "I can't remember what we're looking for," Jad confessed. Thayn had finished examining about half the books.

"I'll recognize it when I see it."

Jad continued leafing through the books at random. He chanced upon many interesting items. Some facts, as a Woodsward, he already knew. The cities, their intent and design. Stories of the Ancient Days.

Other information was new to Jad. The names of other lands. Jad knew only of Kala, and now Vok and Thayn, but there were others, older and distant, and some yet to come. Jad couldn't understand how such information was possible.

Within a Forbidden Book, Thayn had yet to find

anything that he sought.

*

The next morning Cyrll came to them. Thayn and Jad had just returned from the city. Thayn's search of the Forbidden Room was nearly exhausted. So were he and Jad. They almost fell asleep as Cyrll shared with them his intentions.

He proposed that Jad return to a full cycle of duty. Thayn would resume captains' training. It was important, Cyrll explained, to maintain a routine.

Thayn and Jad masked their powers from Cyrll's thoughts. Nor did they betray their recent activities. Jad never doubted that they acted according to the greater will of Kala and Thayn didn't talk about it.

Jad would serve as sentry at a post near the fringe of the Ring. Then he would tend to the berry patches. Finally he would assist in the distribution of foodstuffs. The tour of duty was standard. Meanwhile, if Thayn applied himself, he would finish the first segment of captains' training by the time Jad completed his initial cycle. Then they would have time off together.

*

From the top of a young tree Jad watched the grasslands. The powers that Thayn shared with him allowed Jad to see aspects of light and shadow that he had never appreciated. The movement of the wind was soothing and hypnotic.

*

Thayn looked across the table at the other apprentices. They were older Woodswarder. Captains' training for one so young, Thayn reminded himself, was an honor. He knew what he needed to do. He needed to be respectful of his peers. He needed to consider not *what* he knew – but what he *ought* to know – otherwise he might betray the extent of his powers.

The other Woodswarder in captains' training had been hard at work all the time that Thayn had been away. Despite early attempts to pace himself, Thayn easily – and too obviously – caught up with them. Already ahead in his progress toward goals, he started to skip sessions.

While Jad was on duty, Thayn explored the Ring. As he made his way along various footpaths he studied the Woodswarder overhead. He climbed after them. A network of broad branches and bridging formed alternate avenues throughout the Ring.

Thayn traveled through the canopy. Vaults opened and closed above him, leafy clouds drifting in a great green sky. He felt fierce regret for lost and unrecoverable opportunities.

Despite Thayn's recent journeys and seclusion after returning to Eator, the other Woodswarder all knew him – or *of* him. They hailed him from their posts and greeted him on the paths. Thayn surprised the patrons of several clearings with a visit.

Many clearings were well known for acrobatics or aerial work. Some were devoted to other recreation. A few, tucked away in the deepest shadows, were seldom discussed. The hidden hollows.

Thayn had never visited one, but he didn't hesitate now. It was quiet, grown close with thick and stunted trees that branched low from twisting trunks.

A young man wearing white bristlecloth through his belt appeared on the opposite side of the hollow. He pulled at his curly blond hair and looked around.

Thayn asked his companions, "Who's this?"

Every young man who passed through the Second Door earned tenure as a Woodsward by attending to his First Task. It challenged him to explore and greet his fellows. The ritual allowed for a measured transition to the Ring. Other activities would wait.

"He's on his First Task," a Woodsward realized. He called to the young man, "You shouldn't be here."

The young man withdrew into the trees. Several of the others laughed.

"First Task, of course," Thayn whispered.

*

Although it was difficult, Thayn and Jad managed to visit the Forbidden Room almost every night. At last Thayn angrily slammed the final book shut.

Jad asked, "Didn't find what you're looking for – here?"

Thayn flashed Jad an angry look, mimicking him, "No, I didn't find what – *here*? Did you say 'here'?"

"Yes."

Thayn's expression changed. "Yes – perhaps there are other places. Other sources."

"Sources?"

"Other books of knowledge and power," Thayn considered. "Who would know about them?"

Jad thought of Jovia and Elyda, but they were both dead. "Yara, I suppose."

"Yara." Thayn stood still for a moment and almost closed his eyes. It was as if, by means of his concentration, he was reading something far away. His expression relaxed and his eyes opened. "No, Yara's an idiot."

"Thayn," Jad objected.

"It *has* to be here." Thayn brought his fist down on a counter.

"Thayn, calm down."

He flashed Jad another angry look, then checked himself. "You're right, yes. I've missed something. I'll begin again." He pulled a book from the highest shelf.

"I'm so tired," Jad complained.

"Take a nap. You're no help."

Thayn's words would have been hurtful had they not rung true. "All right." Jad *didn't* feel helpful. He sat on the floor with his head against a shelf.

As Jad fell asleep, Thayn pulled a second book down next to the first one, reviewing them simultaneously, and then a third.

*

The next afternoon a steward intercepted Thayn on his way to a hidden hollow. "Cyrll wants to know why you aren't in captains' training."

"Tell Cyrll I already know all I need to know."

The steward closed his eyes and, in a whisper, repeated Thayn's words. Then he opened his eyes and informed Thayn, "Cyrll wants to see you – now."

Thayn reported to the pavilion. Cyrll stood. No captains were with him and the steward withdrew. "Tell me what I want to know."

Thayn hesitated. "I don't understand." Cyrll narrowed his eyes and Thayn averted them.

"Why aren't you in captains' training?"

"I've finished my assignments."

"Indeed?" Cyrll smiled doubtfully.

"Is there a test?" Thayn asked.

"You're ready for the test? I don't think it's possible – "

"I am."

Thayn's attitude challenged Cyrll's will. "Very
well." He declined his head.

Thayn's mind filled with Cyrll's questions. His
face slackened.

At first Cyrll feared that he had damaged Thayn.
Instead, squinting, Thayn filled the High Warden's
mind with answers, all of them correct, followed by
several questions of his own.

Cyrll brought his hands to his temples. "Oh." He
lost awareness for a moment.

Pulling off his withered wreath, Cyrll shook his
head. White locks fell into place and he returned his
crown. "We need to talk. Sit, please."

Unwillingly, Thayn sat. He had other business.

Cyrll considered his words carefully. "You know
quite a bit. More, perhaps, than is in your best interest.
Knowledge, unless tempered by wisdom, amounts to

neither."

Thayn turned his head. Derisively, he moved his lips with Cyrll's words.

"Together," Cyrll continued, "knowledge and wisdom are a redoubtable combination. Captains' training, Thayn, is about more than knowledge. Its greatest component is the collegiality it offers."

Thayn closed his eyes and rolled them.

"In time, you'll master collaborative skills. You'll embrace models of distributed leadership. These abilities come only with experience. They're essential if you're to serve as High Warden someday."

"High Warden?" Thayn's eyes opened wide.

A smile played upon Cyrll's lips. "Will you return to training?"

Thayn considered this new piece of information. He decided, "Yes."

"And your knowledge – keep it to yourself until the others in training have the opportunity to acquire it for themselves. Discovery, you see, is a key to authenticity."

"I promise." Thayn kneeled quickly, paying his respects, and took leave of Cyrll.

*

It was the last day of Jad's duty as a scout. He was

already tired. The next phase of his cycle, tending the berry patches, would begin early the next morning. He dropped from the trees on his way home and followed several Woodswarder along a busy path. He overheard their conversation.

"Thayn? When?"

"Every time I've been there lately."

"What happens in the hidden hollows?"

"You've never been – ? But we don't speak of it. Come."

CHAPTER SIXTEEN
A visit home

Thayn had been seen in the hidden hollows? Jad thought about the Woodsward's words and fought back the panic that comes with confusion. How could it be true? Something had come over him since their return from the desert, but Jad had attributed it to the powers of Kala. Their regression was debilitating, as Cyrll reminded him – and then Thayn's powers came back.

In response, Jad wondered, to what?

He ducked to glance into their bower and was relieved to find it empty. He wasn't sure what he'd say to Thayn right now. He'd never felt this way.

Jad paced, wondering how he could be suspicious of Thayn. He was never upset by anything that Thayn said or did, especially lately. He expected that Thayn would never fail at anything – or fail him – that's what Jad thought – until now.

He took a few steps, turned around and took them back again, thinking. How tired he was – and Thayn must be – almost every night visiting the Forbidden Room on top of daily duty and captains' training. Exhausted, had Thayn simply taken a wrong turn and lost his way?

No – who was Jad kidding? He needed to face the facts. But the *hidden hollows*? It was as if Jad didn't know Thayn anymore – or himself.

A voice in his head attempted to assure Jad that everything was as it should be. He climbed a tree and watched the approaching ways. Was that Thayn? No, just someone else on the path.

Yes – that was it, Jad decided. That Woodsward was wrong. He had mistaken Thayn for someone else, surely.

But everyone knew Thayn.

More conflicted than ever, Jad considered his options. He could either be angry or hurt. Of the two, he chose the former.

*

The sun slowly set. Light slanted through breaks in the canopy. Shadows pooled together and faded as the Ring took on a glow of its own.

Jad could endure waiting no longer. He decided to

visit the hidden hollows himself.

At first he had trouble finding any of them. More than once Jad lost his sense of direction. Thayn wasn't among those in the first hollow that he located, or the second.

At the entry of every hollow an attendant required Jad to recite a pledge of secrecy. Those in the hollows hailed him. Jad continued his search without success. He finally asked a group of Woodswarder directly if anyone knew Thayn.

"Of course."

"Who doesn't?"

"Is he here?"

"Not now."

"I saw him earlier in another hollow."

"Where?"

"I can't remember."

Several other Woodswarder shared that they had seen Thayn in hidden hollows all over the Ring. Jad left without another word.

*

The moon rose and climbed into the sky. Jad had returned to their bower. Still Thayn wasn't there. Jad sat, resolved to wait. His chin lowered to his chest and jerked up at the sound of the wind. He tried not to fall asleep.

At last, a twig outside the bower snapped. Thayn arrived, slipping through the shadows. He opened several baskets along the wall, looking for something. "Don't worry about disturbing me," Jad announced.

"You're awake?" Thayn sounded out of breath.

"It's late. Where have you been?"

After a moment that was much too long, Thayn replied, "I've been exploring."

"Really?"

"Yes, and analyzing our situation through the eyes of our enemy. We're susceptible."

"Are we?"

"There are weaknesses in our defense."

"Of which you can speak?"

A wind rattled the Ring. Under the sound of the leaves, Jad heard a whisper. It grew louder, calling Jad from the city. A sudden sensation brought his fingertips to his temples.

"Jad?" Thayn asked.

"I – "

"You hear it, don't you?"

"Yes," Jad whispered. The sensation overpowered Jad's thoughts of anything else.

"Strong, isn't it?"

"We better go."

"I'm ready," Thayn agreed. He carried with him a pouch that he retrieved from a basket. "Come."

They hurried to the nearest sector gate, which was open, and along the outer path to the city. Again they visited the Forbidden Room. Thayn no longer made any attempt to conceal from Jad the true extent of his powers.

Jad held his head between his hands. The room swirled as books fell from the shelves and cluttered the counter. Their jackets opened and their pages turned by themselves. Thayn closed his eyes and whispered, reading.

*

Two Woodswarder ambled along a trail in the under-brush, a shortcut between major paths through the Ring. The first Woodsward tripped over something. They laughed until the second Woodsward noticed what it was. A foot. They pulled a limp body from the bushes.

"Is he conscious?"

"He's dead." A young man with curly blond hair stared up at them.

*

The shelves of the Forbidden Room emptied. The

counter was stacked with books, many of them open. Their pages fluttered, then fell to rest. A second scan yielded nothing. "It's not here," Thayn wailed. He beat his hand against his forehead and pulled at his hair. He had reviewed countless bits and pieces of arcane knowledge.

The swirling sensation in Jad's head subsided as the books grew still. He looked at Thayn. Somehow he appeared almost pitiable. "Is it – ?" Jad hesitated. The last time that he questioned him, Thayn became angry.

"Is it what?" Thayn asked, obviously attempting to be tolerant, his voice edgy.

"Perhaps – " Jad chose his words carefully " – you aren't finding what you're looking for because it's not here."

"But where else could it be? I've searched every-where."

"On that page, maybe, that's torn out."

Thayn hadn't paid attention to how Jad spent their time together in the Forbidden Room. Jad, too, had looked through the books, but in a cursory way, noting different aspects of them. "Torn out?"

"Missing."

Thayn's expression changed. At first he seemed to

look at nothing. He slowly grew more animated. "A missing page? Yes – what's on it? Tell me," Thayn demanded.

"How can I? It's missing."

"Which book?"

"It's right – " Jad reached up to an empty shelf. Books lay everywhere on the counter. He took a fearful step away from Thayn. "I don't remember."

Thayn clenched his fist and raised his arm. Then his eyes widened and his hands flew to his head.

"What do you feel?" Jad asked.

"Feel? It's nothing I *feel*. I *know*." He ran his hand across his brow, absently plucking a hair from his head. "He has it. Yes. *He* does."

"Who?"

Thayn hurried out of the Forbidden Room. He ran through the library and into the Great Path.

Jad followed. "Thayn. Wait."

*

It would soon be morning. Jad barely could make Thayn out as he entered the nexus across from the marketplace. Finally he caught up with him.

Again Thayn and Jad violated the laws of the city by going among the Genexus. Of what purpose their visit was this time, Jad didn't know. "Where are you going?" Thayn hesitated as if sensing his way.

He stopped in front of an imposing dwelling with a partial second story that reached up along the wall of an outer path. "This is it." From its description Jad recognized the household of Thayn's family. Without knocking, they opened the door and entered.

*

The body of the young Woodsward was taken to Cyrll who communicated with the Woodsward's mentor, an old steward who quickly joined them.

He looked at Cyrll, confused. "What happened?"

Cyrll shook his head. "We know nothing."

The old man wept.

"Unless, perhaps – " Cyrll remembered Thayn's recent display of arcane knowledge " – there's someone who can help us."

He closed his eyes, concentrating. Cyrll searched the Ring in thought. He couldn't find Thayn in any sector. In turn, he sought out Jad.

Opening his eyes, Cyrll looked toward the Wooden Wall, puzzled. He sensed Jad in the city.

*

Thayn's childhood home had expanded as his family grew. His mother remarried after Zayn's so-called accident. Nor did Kalia find comfort in her new husband, Dirak. Instead she enjoyed the attention of an older neighbor, Daloth, who lived nearby with his un-happy wife and two daughters. His wife, Jiara, and Dirak fell in love as Daloth consoled Kalia. Everyone remarried. Daloth and Jiara's daughters, Ava and Eril, joined Thayn's household, but now Daloth and Kalia, and Dirak and Jiara, were husband and wife. A nurse, Zylla, came to care for Zayn and they, to everyone's surprise, married, too. All the women had children by their new partners. As the eldest husband, Daloth was head of the household, a Senior Peer.

A primary precept of the city was preservation of the family unit for the sake of the children. As a result, some families grew large, although from time to time even a childless couple would remain together for life. Every schoolchild of Eator had been taught the princi-ples of family structure and stability.

Thayn's was a model household. Jad looked at its main room. The walls had been broken out more than once, leaving only the corners, and additional rooms had been built around them.

Thayn turned around several times. Jad watched uncomprehendingly. He returned Thayn to the mo-ment by asking, "Why are we here?"

As if he were a stranger, Thayn scowled at Jad,

then studied the room again. "It has to be here." Low tables and benches sat about the room and, in recesses, looms. The walls were decorated with colorful weavings. In the corners were crannies and shelves laden with books. Thayn rifled through them.

"Hush." Jad stepped around a corner as someone entered the room.

"Who's there?" asked a soft voice. It belonged to Eril. She was almost a woman now.

"Go to bed." Thayn turned his back on her, disguising his voice.

"Dirak?" Eril asked. Her hair was as red as Ava's, but bushy. "Is that you?"

"Yes," Thayn replied. He whispered quick words under his breath.

"What are you doing?"

His whispering continued. "Go to bed," Thayn repeated aloud.

"But – "

"Go, I said."

Eril stopped. Her voice lost inflection. "As you wish." She obeyed, turned around and started back the way that she had come.

"Eril? Are you all right?" came a voice from down the hall.

"Dirak?"

"Is someone with you?"

"I – oh – " Eril's startle was stronger than Thayn's spell. Looking back at him, she screamed.

*

Earlier Cyrll felt something unfamiliar in a corner of his thinking. It was strong, but Cyrll was a Woods-ward of profound discipline and his mind was his own. He held a fingertip to the side of his head and created a hasty partition.

Pain swelled behind it now.

Where did it come from, this unfamiliar thought? Cyrll reviewed his recent activity.

Thayn – the captain's test.

And now he couldn't locate Thayn in his thoughts and Jad was in the city. Why? Cyrll had to alert Yara. He communicated with her in thought.

Yara awoke. She sat up in bed and cast her con-templation throughout the city. The Hall of Choosing was undisturbed. The ways within the Center were all quiet. She sensed, however, that an important door had been opened, and not by her.

A breach of the Forbidden Room? "No." It was impossible. Yara sprang from bed and, grabbing a robe, hurried out of her chamber.

Cyrll cautioned Yara not to be foolhardy. He requested that she and her Monitors wait for him and his captains. It was their responsibility as Woodswarder to protect them.

*

Dirak hurried to Eril, followed by Jiara who reacted quickly to her daughter's scream. They stood staring at Thayn.

Daloth appeared, demanding, "What's the meaning of this?"

"But it's not – " Eril squinted, dazed.

"Thayn?" Daloth asked.

Zylla and Kalia hurried into the room carrying the little ones. Neela and Zod were with them. Thayn collapsed to the floor, slumping against the wall.

"Thayn," Kalia cried. She handed Lo to Jiara and rushed to his side. "Thayn, what are you doing here? What's happened to you? Are you all right? Speak to me."

Confusion increased as Jad, unable to check his concern, appeared around the corner. The others, astonished, stared at him. Jiara and Zylla took a step backwards.

"Who are you?" Daloth demanded. Thin locks of gray hair hung the wrong way from his head, exposing his baldness.

Thayn lay at their feet the same way that he lay in the grass outside Eator when Cyrll and Tylos approached. Again Jad looked down at him, confused. "What's wrong?"

Thayn's eyes were almost closed.

Daloth stepped toward him. "Thayn, who is this young man? Why are you here in the middle of the night? What's the meaning of this?"

The last member of the household to join them was Zayn. Jad was amazed how much Thayn looked like his father.

"You have it, don't you?" Thayn's voice sounded strange.

Daloth looked back and forth between Thayn and Zayn. "This is foolishness. Are you asking *him*?" he snorted.

Kalia brushed the hair off Thayn's brow. "He's not well," she protested.

"I don't understand." As if rousing from a dream, Jad objected, "Thayn, this isn't right. What – ?"

Glancing between Jad and Daloth, Thayn inclined his arm and pointed a finger. In response to his whisperings, Jad grew silent and expressionless.

Daloth continued to ask questions. "Why don't the

Monitors accompany you? Does Yara know you're here? Why do you look different to me? We'll call the Monitors. If all is as it should be, fine. If not, then we'll see. Dirak, help me raise him to his feet."

"No, you *won't*." A tone of voice unheard in years filled the room. Zayn's voice. It was expressive and forceful. His mind was reopened.

Zayn grabbed Dirak's arm and twisted it behind his back, restraining him. Thayn scrambled to his feet, holding Kalia by the wrist.

Daloth stared at the others in disbelief. He was never disobeyed. He didn't know what to do.

"Thayn," Kalia objected. "You're hurting me."

*

Cyrll and his captains raced into the city. Yara and her Monitors were waiting. "Good," Cyrll acknowledged them, nodding. He and his captains adjusted their robes. The Monitors hurried to the archway of Thayn's nexus, Yara and the Woodswarder following them. They hurried up its narrow, crooked pathways.

The Monitors knew Thayn's household well. They had been called to escort Zayn to the High Minister on more than one occasion.

Cyrll held Jad in his thinking. He wasn't far away. Jad's mind, although guarded, was easy for Cyrll to locate. Then, all of a sudden, it was gone.

*

Dirak struggled with Zayn who, as if unaware of what he was doing, easily restrained him. Kalia cried. Daloth attempted to release her from Thayn's grip, again demanding, "What's the meaning of this?"

"Don't touch me." Thayn stepped backwards, taking Kalia with him. His face contorted. He spoke to Daloth in a voice that seethed with hatred and rage. "Old man, I don't like you."

PART FOUR

CHAPTER SEVENTEEN
Another homecoming

"Why was my son taken?" Arlos' mother asked the jury of pillars in the Archive of Time. Recovered from her swoon, she pointed at Thayn. "Why not him?"

"He suggests the taking of our son was *his* punishment?" Arlos father laughed.

"It's *our* punishment," his mother lamented.

"He's taken our son twice. Why not punish *him*?"

Arlos mother sobbed and wept.

Thayn wept, too. He looked around the Archive. "Punish me, yes. Let me exchange places with Arlos."

Kala looked down at the two piles of sand. "At the moment, it would make no difference."

"You ask, 'Why not him?'" Lor, as Thayn's mentor and advocate, inquired of Arlos' mother. "Consider this testimony." At Lor's bidding various pillars of the Archive of Time presented a series of appearances.

* Chapter Seventeen *

Vok led his army of Outcasts through the Third Door of Yutor. Few adults fled with their lives and the children were enslaved.

In Eator, Thayn stood before the Doors of Choosing and pointed at the Third Door. "I hear – crying. The crying of children."

As depicted by the pillars and narrated by Lor, Thayn's history continued. After liberating Yutor, he visited the temple of Kala and the land of Vok. After rescuing the stolen youth of Kala, he wandered the desert seemingly forever until he fell through a whirlpool of sand and into his present situation.

"Thayn offers to take your son's place, to sacrifice himself," Lor addressed Arlos' parents. "Let me show you the consequence of such an untimely exchange."

The pillars redefined themselves. Arlos and his new wife, Glenna, along with the greater population of Eator, lay slain in the pathways of the city. Vok stood over them, unchecked and laughing.

"No," Arlos' mother wailed.

The Archive returned to itself. "That's all." Lor's argument was complete.

Again sobbing, Arlos' mother stared at Thayn. At last she reached out her hands to him, apologetic.

Arlos' father hung his head, silent.

The jury spoke. "Arlos is dead. For that there is no remedy. Wouldn't it be better, for the sake of his parents, for him never to have existed? It would spare them pain."

"Don't deprive Arlos of the memory he deserves," Thayn protested. He spoke directly to Arlos' parents, "I know his passing is painful. I won't tell you I share your pain, but I respect it. I ask the same of you. My pain is my own. It would be greater still if it were taken from me. We must guarantee Arlos' existence in order to honor it."

Arlos' mother continued to sob, a soft throaty cry. Arlos' father took her hand, nodding sadly at Thayn.

"Where," asked the jury, "is this one called Vok?" The Archive shuddered. A pillar not far from Thayn assumed a contorted shape. The members of the jury gasped and whispered among themselves.

"How horrible. Evil has been among us all along."

"He's the guilty one. How didn't we know?"

"Touch him," the jury ruled. He doesn't deserve to exist."

Touch him – really? The sense of rightness that he shared with his mother prompted Thayn to ask himself, "Can it be this easy? Or is this too good to be true?" His questions deflected a greater sense of foreboding.

The jury's previous suggestion that Arlos cease to exist was a reckless one. Wasn't this the same recommendation? Thayn objected, "But without Vok's existence, Arlos' death has no meaning. Don't you see what you're wishing away? Don't you understand?"

Arlos' parents regarded each other searchingly. After a moment they nodded at the jury of pillars. Their faces faded. The other pillars returned to their original smooth, symmetrical shape.

The room tilted. The Archive of Time and Thayn turned upside down. Although the existing pillars appeared no different, the two piles of sand that rested at Thayn's feet spilled and themselves reformed into pillars, hardening. Again they supported the great chamber, one of the Dead and the other of the Living.

The ceiling opened under Thayn's feet and he fell through it.

*

Thayn awoke on the desert. He groaned. How long had he been drifting? The morning was cold and he was thirsty. He stood on shaky legs.

In the distance he saw a familiar body of land. It was closer than the horizon and not a hallucination. Clouds crowned Kala and within them Thayn could see flashes of light.

The clouds broke away and spread over Thayn. Warm rain fell. Thayn tilted back his head and the water splashed against his tongue. It tasted sweet.

He continued to walk home.

*

Kalia looked up at her former husband as he was before his so-called accident, not a mere shell of himself, expressionless and silent. The rest of the household stared in astonishment, except Dirak, who struggled to free himself. Without thinking, Zayn slammed Dirak into the wall.

"Dirak?" Jiara cried.

"What are you – ?" Kalia cried. "My arm."

Zayn shook himself and looked around the room. At the sight of Kalia his face broke into a spontaneous grin. It remained only for a moment.

Kalia resisted Thayn's grip. She looked into unfamiliar eyes and took a quick breath. "This isn't – " Her tone changed and she hesitated.

"See here – " Daloth stepped forward again.

" – my son," Kalia warned them.

A bright bolt of light sprang from Thayn's fingertips and Daloth reeled. An even brighter bolt knocked everyone to the floor as the door burst open. Woodswarder and Monitors sprang into the room.

Warning and rescue came too late. The little ones cried and Jiara and Zylla crawled to them. Eril, Neela and Zod hugged one another. Dirak pulled himself to his feet. Thayn, Zayn and Jad were gone.

Kalia knelt next to her husband. She whispered to herself, repeating her warning, but Daloth was dead.

*

Thayn, Zayn and Jad reappeared in the Hall of Choosing. Zayn rubbed his forehead. Jad blinked at them, expressionless, as Thayn studied the room. Wall by wall he pressed his palms against the stone. With his fingertips he quickly and methodically examined every portion of it.

The Doors of Choosing trembled at Thayn's touch. Again he sought something that he couldn't find.

Ministration approached. With quick words Thayn provoked open the Second Door. He and Zayn appeared in the pavilion of the Ring.

Zayn looked around in wonder at the headquarters of the High Warden. Despite its natural glow, Thayn suggested, "Let's see this better."

A bolt of light escaped his fingertips. "Oh," Zayn exclaimed as sparks traveled up the gnarlwood. The canopy reached high overhead, a fluttering ceiling.

The gnarlwood burst into flame.

Thayn lamented in an exaggerated whisper, "Alak. Now, let's go," he cried. Zayn followed him out of the pavilion, through the trees and into the grasslands.

His laughter raced on the wind.

*

Yara examined Daloth. She shook her head and stood. "There's nothing I can do. I'm sorry."

Kalia sobbed. Zylla attempted to embrace her.

Eril took the children to her room. Dirak, unexpectedly having become the Senior Peer of the household, paced up and down the hall. The Monitors and Woodswarder stood in attendance.

Cyrll held a hand to his head. He concentrated, searching for Thayn, but could elicit nothing in response. Everyone looked expectantly at him. "Thayn and his father evade me, but I sense Jad – barely. He's in the Hall of Choosing."

Jiara handed him an open pouch that she found on the floor. "What's this?" Cyrll pulled from the pouch the white bristlecloth of a young Woodsward.

*

From a perch high in a towering tree Yodin looked down the mountain slope to the desert. He guarded the clearing of the Green Folk. Others of his fellowship were embedded elsewhere among the trees.

* Chapter Seventeen *

A disturbance in the canopy suggested that something, or someone, was coming his way. Thayn fell from the trees. Yodin found him curled up on the forest floor, burnt by the sun and sand, shaking. He was barely conscious.

Why, Yodin speculated, was Thayn here again – and in such bad shape? Something was wrong, Yodin was sure of it, but he no longer expected Thayn to offer him an explanation. On his last visit Thayn had treated Yodin no differently than any other of his folk.

Thayn whispered, his eyes blinking, "Yodin, is that you?" An undeniable expression of recognition played upon his face, then slackened as Thayn succumbed to unconsciousness. Yodin wasn't sure what to do.

*

Thayn awoke. As on his first visit, he was secured in a cradle of roots that grew from a wall cut into a hillside of the mountain. Branches had broken Thayn's fall from the treetops and he was only bruised. His surroundings, this time, were a comfort to him.

Yodin brought him a healing brew of idleflower. Unprompted, Thayn drank it. Yodin, for some reason, wasn't speaking directly to him. Thayn listened to Yodin's conflicted thoughts.

What, he wondered, had he done to offend Thayn?

Yodin tried not to think about it.

Thayn didn't understand Yodin's change in behavior. Of all the Green Folk, Yodin was the only one whose thoughts made any sense to him.

Yodin was upset and, despite attempts to keep his thinking to himself, emotions painted pictures in his mind. Moreover, Thayn had become an astute communicator. Yodin had yet to look Thayn in the eye and already his mind was open to him.

Thayn grew concerned as Yodin recollected details of his recent visit. Why, Yodin wondered, had Thayn ignored him? His thoughts included another Woodsward.

"Jad?" Thayn asked aloud.

His question confused Yodin. Hadn't they, Thayn and Jad, left the clearing of the Green Folk together? Yodin remembered the particulars of Jad and Thayn's earlier visit, their reunion and tribute.

Thayn explored Yodin's thoughts, regarding them as pieces of a puzzle to put together. What was it that he would figure out?

The solution came to Thayn with a sickening sensation. He shook his head. "No." Someone else, he realized, had already come to the clearing of the Green Folk, someone who looked quite a bit like him. And he had left with Jad? If so, then –

Yodin looked at Thayn curiously. Thayn needed to explain his suspicions to Yodin, but how? He held a hand above his face and looked at Yodin, smiling. As he lowered his hand to his chin he grimaced, contorting his face. He raised his hand, smiling again.

Yodin didn't understand.

What was their name for him? Thayn heard it on his first visit to the clearing, a guttural sound. Yodin had gestured a slash to his throat, asking if Vok's death was Thayn's goal. At the time Thayn's answer was "yes."

Now Thayn made the guttural sound as best he remembered, gesturing the slash to his throat and shaking his head.

Yodin, at last, understood. "You didn't kill him?" he wondered.

"No." Thayn shook his head again. As on his first visit to the clearing of the Green Folk, he was challenged to communicate complex ideas to another without a common language. Again the solution was the wall that, cut into the hillside, exposed roots that fashioned the cradle in which Thayn lay. The wall was flat and moist. Using his fingertip, Thayn sketched upon it, communicating with Yodin through pictures.

"You?" the Green One asked in response to the first figure that Thayn drew.

Thayn nodded. He drew two figures over the first one.

"Parents?"

Nodding again, Thayn pointed to one of the parents, then back and forth between Yodin and himself.

"Father?"

"Yes." Above them Thayn drew two more figures.

"Grandparents?"

"You're good at this, Yodin." Below these new figures, next to his father, Thayn drew one last shape. Again he pointed back and forth between Yodin and himself.

Yodin shook his head, confused.

Thayn pointed to the last shape, and to the figure of his father, and again lowered and raised his hand over his face, changing his expression.

Yodin reviewed the drawings until his yellow eyes grew wide. He freed Thayn from the cradle and beckoned him to follow. They made their way unobserved to the clearing of Yodin's folk, keeping within a deep shadow of the trees. Yodin pointed at – what?

Except for their smiles they looked like saplings. Thayn and Yodin watched two boys at play. The same shade of green, they were identical to the eye. Twins.

"Yes," Thayn whispered, nodding. They returned to the hillside and, again, Thayn referred to the figures that he had drawn. He pointed to his father and to the last shape, his father's twin.

Yodin nodded.

Then Thayn brought his meaning together, making three gestures and one sound. He began with the slicing gesture, shaking his head, and with the other hand he pointed to the last figure again. He attempted the guttural sound.

Thayn sensed incomprehension on Yodin's part. He understood Thayn's gestures separately, but not together. Yodin reviewed all the drawings, remembering each one, thinking aloud, "You – parents – father – grandparents – "

Slowly Yodin's expression changed. Raising his hands to his mouth, revelation by revelation, he puzzled everything out.

Thayn waited until –

" – uncle," Yodin cried. Horror flooded his mind as he realized all that happened. Accepted among his folk? Presented to the Old One? Yodin looked at Thayn, asking him to confirm his darkest thoughts.

Thayn nodded and whispered, "Vok." The wind

howled in the trees. How was this possible?

*

Yodin had yet to share the news of Thayn's arrival with any other Green Folk. He sensed that something was amiss and had attended to Thayn in secret. Based on what he learned, he decided to share his news with Tadin, the Old One, now. Thayn, meanwhile, rested in the cradle after another dose of idleflower brew.

*

Yodin returned quickly with unanticipated news. "Tadin wants you to leave."

"What?"

"Immediately. Follow me." Yodin's sense of urgency alarmed Thayn, who complied. They skirted the clearing. Yodin thought freely as they traveled knowing again that Thayn would understand him. "Tadin fears that, once deceived, nothing will protect us from further deception."

"He mistrusts you. I argued with him, but he dismissed me." The idleflower thinned in patches behind them. "And I spoke recently with my friends among the Blue Folk. They told me you – the *other* you, I mean – and your friend were also received by the city in the lake. The Dyad welcomed them. This is bad. They'll hear of the deception. They're less forgiving than Tadin."

In time they reached the edge of a sheer cliff and carefully descended. Yodin had a plan. "We need to find my friend Alwala. You rode him to the Well of Understanding. Together we'll form a pact.

"In defense of my folk, within our mountain clearing, I will obey Tadin." They climbed down into the foothills. "From where we stand now, I question him. Together we must work against this evil. Alwala will transport you home.

"We'll share an invocation and a password, a way to call and recognize one another. Let's think."

Thayn and Yodin left the trees and descended the grassy slopes to the lake. The Blue One was waiting. Yodin called to him.

His head bobbed out of the water. He told Thayn, "I regret I missed your visit to our city. I was upriver when – " Hearing the thoughts of Yodin and Thayn, Alwala stopped short. His understanding of the situation was immediate.

It was worse than Yodin feared. The Blue Folk detested duplicity and would shun all players associated with Vok's deception, even Thayn. It wasn't fair, but such was the result of evil.

They must act quickly, Alwala warned them. He

would provide Thayn transportation before access to the lake was denied him. They agreed upon "Kalala" as a call. As a secret signal "palms together" would be their password and gesture.

Thayn thanked Yodin and, with a shiver, slipped into the lake. Alwala pulled him down into the water and secured him in place. They sliced through choppy shallows, the Blue One navigating a course directly to the river, avoiding the city.

Surrendering himself to the bubbling water through which they twirled and the blue of the sky, Thayn remembered little of his journey upriver. Alwala delivered him somersaulting to the grassy bank before they reached Tordawn. Each raising a hand, palms together, Thayn thanked the Blue One. Alwala wished him well and, without a splash, disappeared.

Thayn heard a squeak. Only a few rats chased him and he quickly outran them. He eased his pace, looking around, turning full circle and orienting himself. Scattered woods grew everywhere. In the distance he sensed Eator.

He decided that he wouldn't go there – at least, not yet. It wasn't fair that he was punished for his uncle's transgressions, he reasoned, but it would be even worse if he didn't learn from them. For what deed of Vok might he be punished next, he wondered – if he wasn't careful? Thayn needed time to think.

He headed for the nearby highlands. Up into them thinning grass climbed the ribs of Kala to become open meadows surrounded by stands of slender trees. Thayn aimed for a crag that he remembered spotting while on sentry duty in Eator. A recess within it would offer him protection from the eye and the elements. Thayn leapt up a tumble of rock and gazed out over the grass-lands. Staring down at the Ring of Eator, he surren-dered himself to his troubled thoughts.

Thayn reviewed all the news that Yodin and Al-wala had shared. He continued to fear the worst, but he wasn't exactly sure what the worst might be. If Vok visited Eator disguised as himself – Thayn didn't want to think about it, but he couldn't think about anything else.

Night fell. The moon rose bright over the moun-tains. Thayn fell into a fitful sleep.

*

At dawn a huge cloud approached Eator. Already a plume of smoke drifted over the city. It came from the smithies, Thayn assumed. He yawned and rubbed his eyes. Under the smoke Thayn saw a lick of flame. It came from the far side of the city. It was the Ring –

on fire.

Thayn scrambled down the hillside and sprinted across the thin stretch of grasslands that separated the mountains from Eator. Disregarding a hail from the trees, he raced into the Ring. He was prepared to greet an interception party. Instead, a blow to the head from behind stunned him.

Monitors waited outside the sector gate. They carried Thayn, barely conscious, to the Center and along a series of passageways. A door opened and the Monitors pushed him through it. The floor disappeared and Thayn fell into the Forgotten Room.

CHAPTER EIGHTEEN
The Forgotten Room

Moments after Daloth's death, in response to communication from Yara, the Ministration secured the Center. Monitors discovered a Woodsward standing in the Hall of Choosing.

He didn't move. They snapped their fingers in his face. Jad stared, unresponsive. His mind was closed.

Yara arrived to examine Jad. He seemed much the same as Daloth, except alive. She held a fingertip to his forehead. "Oh." She pulled away in pain.

*

Cyrll returned to the Ring in response to an urgent call from his captains. A flickering glow already escaped the treetops. The sector gate swung open in advance of Cyrll and he bound through the trees toward the High Camp. Fire licked at the ancient gnarlwood. Woodswarder hurried back and forth from the wash stations with bowls of water. Their work was no match for the growing flames.

Many thoughts came to Cyrll all at once and competed for his attention. Although he wasn't overly sentimental, he was touched by what he saw happening around him.

Every Woodsward entered the Ring ceremoniously through the pavilion. With the opening of the Second Door he was introduced to a new life in support of his city and the culture of Kala. Now Woodswarder stood side by side, passing bowls of sloshing water in a valiant but futile attempt to save their hallowed passage. Resin bubbled from the ancient gnarlwood as, dripping with flame, it crackled and smoked.

As High Warden, Cyrll was conscientious in the fulfillment of his duties. Chiefly by expulsing itinerant Outcasts, he protected Eator. He was well acquainted with the city's constitution and its character. He supported its laws, knew its rules and played by them. His reactions were solid and methodical.

How, in return for all his hard work, could the pavilion be on fire? Flames leapt into the canopy.

Anger intensified Cyrll's strength. He was already a powerful man. Who, he wondered, dared to do this to him? This was not the work of Kala. Cyrll knew that he was undeserving of such a fate. Instead, he sensed great and uncommon evil.

New powers came to Cyrll. He held his hands to the sides of his head. He fought back his responses to what was happening, thoughts of loss, rage and vengeance. Cyrll cleared his mind of them. Drained, he refilled himself with benign willfulness. His blue eyes welled deep. He reached his fingers through his white hair and clenched his hands into fists. His righteous prayer was redirected from the temple of Kala to the surface of the river.

Often hidden in fog, the river carved a steadfast course through the midsection of the land. Cyrll collected its vapors, a heavy mist that lifted into the sky and drifted toward Eator. It reached the Ring, mingling with the light of dawn.

Cyrll's words of prayer became praise as the great cloud billowed above Eator. Woodswarder continued passing bowls of water. The fire crackled.

The cloud descended. There was a great sizzle. The vapor enveloped the canopy and sank, snuffing the gnarlwood.

The Woodswarder cheered.

The pavilion, although scorched, would survive. Cyrll entered the smoldering circle. Several of its aged trunks, however, were beyond hope. They fell outward in a shower of sparks.

Cyrll slumped to the ground. The powers of Kala receded as quickly as they came. Their passing incapacitated the High Warden. Several captains came to him with news of an approaching intruder.

*

Daloth lay on the table in the alcove. Dirak had already bathed him and, with Jiara's help, dressed him in orange, the color of their nexus. Kalia, in black, took her place at his side. Her green eyes were dull. She opened a small drawer in the table and from it withdrew a jar of fragrant ointment. She touched her fingertip to it, then to Daloth's forehead.

She looked across the room. Two husbands had been taken from her. Only Dirak remained, and he belonged to Jiara now. Kalia found little comfort in his sad smile.

Zylla came to her. She experienced such a similar loss that Kalia should have found solace in her company. Without Zayn, however, Zylla meant nothing to Kalia. She endured her embrace for only for a moment before slipping away.

Kalia went to the foot of the table and looked up the length of Daloth. Such a fussy old man – he had provided her with so much security and joy. He was predictable. Kalia easily represented herself around his expectations. He loved her unconditionally. Daloth didn't expect her to make sense – she was a woman – and he was a man of stereotypes. Kalia was practical. They both knew what they were doing. They accepted each other, sharing a sense of cynicism that amused her. Always her green eyes danced, but not now.

Nor did Kalia find any comfort in hearing the news that Daloth's murderer was a prisoner in the Center. The Monitors determined, based upon her previous testimony, that he was Vok.

*

The door closed and with it went the light. The Forgotten Room was deep. There was nothing, for the moment, under Thayn. He wondered, not for the first or last time, if he had fallen into the Abysm.

Far below him, too soon, the floor answered his question. Thayn landed hard at an odd angle. His knee and shoulder screamed in pain. He rolled over, hugging himself until his shoulder eased into place. His knee ached and swelled.

Thayn opened and closed his eyes. He couldn't tell the difference. Everything remained black.

He concentrated, trying to block unrelenting pain,

but he couldn't. He tried to feel nothing at all. That didn't work, either. The floor was strewn with bristle and he pulled it around him as if that might help.

Unseen walls confined his thinking. His thoughts and supplications bounced back and echoed all around him. Thayn dragged himself around the Forgotten Room, feeling his way in the dark. He found food-stuffs, a pile of waterfruit, bread, and a type of stalk that he didn't much like. The bread was flavorless and dry. After sucking on a waterfruit, he threw it through the darkness. He heard it splat against stone.

He didn't understand what was happening to him. He sensed only the injustice. He didn't appreciate his incarceration – this solitude – for what he would later remember it to be – a blessing in disguise. Too soon it would be over.

Thayn drifted in and out of sleep. His knee continued to throb and his shoulder was cold and tight. Sleep and wakefulness blended together. He couldn't separate them.

How much time had passed? It was impossible to tell.

Faint points of light appeared high above in the walls. From them Thayn felt occasional attention. They were spyholes, he reasoned. He wondered who was watching him and in what room they stood.

And this place – how had he never learned of it? He thought that he already knew everything that there was to know – too much – about the city. Here was a feature that he had missed.

What else didn't he know? The question made him laugh. He worried that he knew both too much and too little – what nonsense.

*

A great rain came and went. Daloth was removed to the temple and placed upon a pyre. His funeral was a major event. Daloth was well-respected and many came to honor him. Yara and a delegation of Senior Peers officiated at his service.

Kalia gazed out at the Fallow Field through the statuary that defined the Great Path. Slanting sunlight descended through lingering clouds as the afternoon sky cleared. She watched the shimmering shafts play upon the flowering herb and grasses as she thanked an endless queue of well-wishers for their warm thoughts and condolences.

*

Night settled over Eator. Two gates of the Ring opened on either side of the Fallow Field. One by one the Woodswarder entered and walked along the opposite side of the Wooden Wall past their shrine. They offered respects to a Woodsward who, while on his First Task, met untimely death.

Most had yet to be greeted by him. Never had one so recently arrived – so young – perished. They all shook their heads in sadness.

The Rotation of the Ring took most of the night. The Woodswarder continued walking until they returned to the spot where they had started. The security of the city was uncompromised.

*

Funerals concluded with the strewing of ashes in the Fallow Field. Yara returned to her place behind the dais in the High Chamber. Cyrll tended to the pavilion, pruning the burnt gnarlwood and preparing its branches for propagation. Kalia sat at the table in the alcove, gently stroking the spot where Daloth had lain. They lost themselves in their respective thoughts.

*

For Eator it was a time of rare contemplation. The Genexus considered recent events. First came news of the attack on Yutor. Then a cohort of their youth disappeared. Now Daloth was dead. Everyone spoke of it over breakfast, at work and school, and around the dinner table. The majority of Thayn's nexus attended

Daloth's funeral, joined by Senior Peers from through-out the city.

For some it was a time to reflect on mortality, bles-sings and happiness, a moment in time against which to measure life. For others it was simply sensational – murder among them was rare. Either way, although Daloth himself might soon be forgotten, the uncer-tainty of fate would continue fresh in their thinking.

*

Yara prayed to Kala. She was young and, by the standards of the Ministration, a novice to her station. She came to her office in tumultuous times with much to prove. With Daloth's death the city again was vio-lated. The Forgotten Room confined the guilty party, the perpetrator.

Could it be that easy? Yara struggled to accept her good fortune. Circumspection would be a flaw in her character as High Minister, she decided. She worried that anything she did might be the wrong thing to do. Only by doing nothing, she decided, could she avoid risk. Behaviors of her predecessors made more sense to her, especially those of Elyda.

*

Cyrll mused as he repaired the pavilion. The city was secure, wasn't it? No enemy had breached Eator

246

by force. Only by deception had Vok entered the city.

But Cyrll had welcomed an imposter. The admission was painful. Praise Kala both for a mother's instinct and her keen eye.

Vok had been captured, at least, attempting to enter the city again. He was secure in the Forgotten Room.

Cyrll reviewed the events and their players. Poor Daloth, stubborn to the end. Poor Jad – his was a fate they had yet to reconcile. And Zayn? He wasn't with Vok when they caught him. Cyrll feared, by now, that Outcasts had captured him.

Those were the broad strokes. With further details came specific problems, several of them involving Jad. Cyrll had yet to determine who in the Ring would care for him. In the meantime Jad remained in the Center. Never had a Woodsward of Eator endured his condition.

Complicating matters was the white bristlecloth of the young Woodsward who, while on his First Task, met untimely death. The bristlecloth had been found in Thayn's household. Was Jad an accomplice to another murder – or worse?

*

For several long days and evenings Kalia sat with family and neighbors. She expressed appreciation for all their attention and sympathy. Her heart, however, remained in the Fallow Field among the shafts of sunlight.

*

Thayn sat in the Forgotten Room glumly watching the points of light in the walls overhead. They changed in their intensity from time to time as various thoughts checked in on him. His mind drifting, Thayn wondered yet again if he were in the Abysm, floating with Kala. Or under the night sky in the desert. Or standing in the Archive of Time. "We're in many places at once," Thayn remembered Kala telling him.

Was it Thayn's fate to suffer in all of them? Already he had endured enough, he thought to himself. And this was home.

No, it wasn't fair. This shouldn't be happening to him.

What had his father once said? Something about "shoulds." Thayn couldn't remember. He tried to find comfort in a forgotten memory, but failed.

Thayn paced in the dark, limping a little. He had nothing to do but think. He hated it. He became aware of too many things that he didn't want to know. And too many questions.

Kaden's mission to Yutor, for instance. Was it

part of a plan conceived by Vok? Thayn had attempted to stop Vok's plan, whatever it was. Had he? Or had his actions merely set other events into motion? Others often suggested, "Thayn will figure it out." How sure they were of him. They were wrong.

Thoughts of Kaden persisted. Thayn wondered if Kaden ever, deep down inside, felt like a little boy. Too often, Thayn did.

Thayn could only imagine the scope and sequence of the damage done by Vok. "Oh." He sat on the floor with his head in his hands. What was happening to him?

It was hopeless.

"No," he decided. "I won't live in a world that is hopeless." The simple statement became Thayn's perpetuity.

He prayed.

*

Thayn's prayer was strong. It seeped through the stone and rode away on the wind. His words reached the temple of Kala. Light pooled in the crystal walls until three bright streaks flew free.

Lor, Jovia and Boz sailed between the high and mighty shoulders of Kala and followed the curve of the river to Eator. They circled the Forgotten Room. Its charmed walls repelled them.

Instead they visited the dreams of Cyrll, Yara and Kalia.

*

Lor came to Cyrll. He asked, "Who's been here killing and burning, and who does the Forgotten Room imprison?"

"Vok," Cyrll replied.

"I've asked you two questions. You've given me one answer."

*

"Yara?" Jovia stood to one side of her bed. She also stood to the other side. "Yara?"

There were two Jovias. One of them, Yara sensed, was unreal. She rubbed her eyes and looked at them again.

Both were gone.

*

Kalia slept restlessly. She dreamt in detail of Daloth's murder. Boz appeared and everyone else in her dream stood motionless. "Boz?"

He examined Kalia's captor. "How alike they are, brother and brother, father and son, uncle and nephew. How do you know he isn't Thayn?"

"His eyes," Kalia explained.

There was a great flash of light and everyone but Boz and Kalia was gone. "Now," Boz noted, "he's in the Forgotten Room. Again, how do you know he isn't Thayn?"

"His eyes," Kalia repeated.

"Good. Amazing how they caught him."

Kalia wondered, "Too good to be true?"

"Be careful," Boz cautioned her, "and think. You have to tell the others."

"Others? Tell them what? Boz – ?"

*

"Wake up." Zylla sat at Kalia's bedside, shaking her gently. "You're having a bad dream."

"No," Kalia cried, scolding her. "He was about to tell me what I need – oh – what's *wrong* with you?"

Zylla's face crumpled.

Kalia immediately regretted her harsh words. "I'm sorry, Zylla. I'm not awake."

Zylla sobbed.

"I was dreaming about Thayn. Oh – Zylla, call for the Monitors."

"Monitors?" Zylla wiped her eyes, alarmed.

"I need to speak with Yara. Something is terribly wrong."

CHAPTER NINETEEN
A mother's eyes

Kalia stood before Yara in the High Chamber. Her green eyes narrowed as a measure of her intent. "I wish to see my son."

With a sympathetic smile Yara acknowledged, "Of course, Kalia. We all hope Thayn returns to us safely, and soon."

"Bring him to me."

"I don't understand," Yara replied.

"I wish to see your prisoner."

"But he's not Thayn, he's Vok."

"Is he?"

"It was according to your statement, Kalia, that we incarcerated him."

"I don't question the crimes, or that Vok is responsible for them." Kalia explained, "I question the identity of your prisoner."

Again Yara replied, "I don't understand."

"You brought him here directly from the Ring, un-conscious, so I've heard. I haven't seen him for my-self."

"Are you serious?"

"What if he's Thayn?" Kalia asked.

"What if he isn't?" Yara's tone was grim. "This is dangerous."

Kalia cleared her throat, resolute. "I've a right to see my son."

"As we determine him to be Vok, you've no en-titlement." Yara smiled slightly as Kalia frowned.

"In that case," Kalia amended her request, "I wish to see the murderer of my husband."

They each regarded the other for a moment, both of them interceding on behalf of an interest that they held as dear as life itself, a city and a son. Neither of them blinked. Finally Yara closed her eyes. She held her fingertips to her head, whispering in communica-tion.

Kalia waited and, in time, the door opened. She expected Thayn. Instead, through it, strode the High Warden.

Cyrll threw back the hood of a robe that attempted to disguise him as a Monitor. Kalia looked at him in awe. She barely remembered him from the night of Daloth's death.

"She wishes to see Vok," Yara told him.

"To see if he's Thayn," Kalia explained. "As his High Warden I appeal to you."

Yara continued, "I've told Kalia, according to his identity as Vok, she hasn't the entitlement, but she demands to see him as the murderer of her husband."

Cyrll raised his brow.

"Daloth was a Senior Peer," Kalia told them. "He taught me many useful things. How to tell time by the moon, for instance. And various matters of litigation. It's my right, as a member of the Genexus, to look the murderer of my husband in the eye."

Cyrll looked at Yara.

Yara nodded. She feared, however, releasing the prisoner from the Forgotten Room. She shared her misgivings with Cyrll in thought.

Cyrll deliberated. "We enjoy many rights," he told Kalia, "and some are intended to supersede others. Our greatest right is to safety. Regarding the prisoner, his removal from the Forgotten Room would place us all in jeopardy."

"*If* he's Vok," Kalia agreed. "But of that, Boz and I aren't confident."

"Boz?" Cyrll and Yara asked together.

"He came to me in a dream. He came with a question. He told me to ask you, too."

"What question?"

"'How do you know he isn't Thayn?'"

Cyrll looked from Kalia to Yara and back again. "Lor visited me. I think he asked me the same question, if what you suggest is the answer."

"In my dream two Jovias came," Yara admitted. "I couldn't tell them apart."

Kalia remembered the night of Daloth's death – and Vok. "I looked into his eyes," she whispered. "It was – horrible – I can't describe them. He killed my husband. There was another flash of light and he was gone."

Her tone hardened. She continued, "Gone where? Into the arms of waiting Woodswarder who overpowered him? Is that what happened? Do you really believe you captured Vok without a fight?" she asked Cyrll with a laugh.

Cyrll almost answered, but Kalia continued. "No, there's something wrong. I feel it. With Boz' words I realized – " She hesitated.

"What?" Yara asked.

Kalia collected her thoughts. "In your prison is

either the murderer of my husband, or my son, but not both. Into his eyes, perhaps, I haven't looked."

"We – "

"You worry about the risk," Kalia interrupted. "I know. But if you're wrong – if he's Thayn you imprison – is that a risk worth taking?"

Cyrll and Yara shared an uncomfortable glance.

"I'll spare you the decision. Whether he's Thayn or Vok, by the laws of Eator, I've a right to see him."

*

A lurch and a jerk. Thayn rose into a squat, touching his hands to the floor. He could make out below him the faint turning of a wheel. Was he moving? He listened carefully. He heard a grinding noise, stone against stone.

Thayn stood. Above him the faint points of light lowered, glowing. He turned in a circle. There were more of them than he thought. Without warning, all around him, doors opened. Blinding light streamed through them.

He felt hands everywhere. His arms were jerked this way and that. His head was pulled back and he felt a punch to the stomach. "Oh-h – " A gag slipped into his mouth.

A casing slipped over his head and, again, the

world went black. Bound at the wrists and ankles, he was taken to the High Chamber. He reached out in thought along the way, but no mind would admit him.

*

For a second time Thayn stood on trial. The gag and casing were removed. Again light blinded him.

"Tell us your name."

"Yara? Is that you?"

"Tell us your name," she repeated.

"You know who I am – I'm Thayn. Why are – ?"

"Tell us about your stepfather."

"Daloth? Why, is something wrong?"

"And the fire?" came a new voice.

"Cyrll?"

"The fire?" he repeated.

Thayn told him, "I was in the mountains. I looked down at Eator. There was smoke in the Ring and I ran to tell someone – but somebody must have blindsided me. I woke up in – that place." He tried to rub his shoulder.

"The Forgotten Room."

"What *is* that place? Where am I?" Everything was out of focus and white.

"Tell us about Vok."

"He's taken my form. Is he here?" Thayn asked.

257

"He's come and gone, perhaps," Cyrll said.

"Or perhaps not," Yara added. "If he's capable of taking your form, how do we know?"

"So, it's as Yodin said," Thayn whispered.

"Who?"

"Yodin, the Green One. He said their Old One, Tadin, asked the same question. Alwala, the Blue One, agreed on behalf of his people." As Thayn's eyes grew accustomed to the light he saw shapes in front of him. "I didn't expect the same reception here."

A third figure became visible between the others. Their eyes met. Hers were dull. It took Thayn a moment to recognize them.

"Yes." Her eyes brightened, dancing.

"Mother?"

Kalia raised a hand to her mouth and cried excitedly, "Yes, this is my son."

"Mother? What's happened to you?"

"This is Thayn."

"What about Daloth?" Thayn asked.

"Oh, Thayn, he's dead. By your hand, we thought, but he wasn't you. He was Vok. Then he was imprisoned – but he wasn't Vok – he was you. Boz came to me in a dream. He told me – oh, you must think I'm crazy."

"Oh, Mother, no – I don't."

"He wasn't you."

"Where is he now, Vok?"

"He's gone. We thought he was you. But the way you *held* me – you *hurt* me. You would never hurt me."

"Of course not," Thayn agreed softly. Then he asked Yara and Cyrll, "Where did Vok go?"

"We don't know," Yara sighed.

"He's taken your father," Kalia told him.

"What?" Monitors removed his bonds.

"Zayn – he has Zayn," Kalia repeated.

"I need to stop them."

"How?"

"I'll figure something out. Jad and I will – "

"Oh – " Kalia, Yara and Cyrll said together. Cyrll coughed. Kalia and Yara averted their eyes.

" – put our – " Thayn trailed off. After a moment he asked, "Mother? Cyrll? What's happened?"

Nobody, at first, would answer him. Finally, with resignation Yara called, "Bring him." Ministration escorted Jad into the High Chamber. Thayn immediately recognized his condition.

"No," Thayn cried. He looked at his mother. Always he found comfort in her eyes, but not now. It was Jad's consideration that Thayn sought. He walked to him. Jad looked at nothing, expressionless.

"How is this possible?" Thayn asked.

Jad's face flinched. Everyone in the High Chamber took a quick breath. Jad's eyes flickered for a moment. Without inflection Jad recited haltingly, "Vok – says – you had – your chance."

The flicker was gone. Jad's expression slackened.

Thayn fell to his knees before Yara. "Return me to your Forgotten Room," he whispered.

"No," Kalia cried.

Thayn ran for the door. "Throw me in."

Kalia followed, rushing into his arms. "No, don't leave me."

They sank to the floor in grief and consolation, crying alternately on each other's shoulder or both at the same time. Several cycles of whispers, sad laughter and more crying followed.

Kalia and Thayn refused to part until Yara and Cyrll agreed that they would visit each other daily in the Center. Except for little Lo, Kalia explained to them, Thayn was everything that she had left.

Thayn found Yara and Cyrll in thought. They allowed him access now. Thayn implored, "Permit this, please. I need to be strong for her. She needs me."

First, they would talk with Kalia. There would be terms.

Thayn attended to Jad while the others negotiated. "Jad, can you hear me?" Thayn asked aloud.

Jad stood as if a portrait of his former self.

Thayn kissed him. Jad was unresponsive.

Meanwhile Kalia pleaded her case, whispering, "Permit this, please. I need to be strong for him. He needs me." Yara and Cyrll admired the utility of love between mother and son.

Their business settled, they joined Thayn. Jad answered Thayn's question from several minutes ago. "Yes." His reactions were delayed and his speech was slurred, but he could still communicate.

"How is this possible?" Thayn asked again. "What happened? Tell me."

Cyrll and Yara opened their minds fully. Thayn learned all that had happened since his uncle's arrival. Vok's deception. His rifling of the Forbidden Room. Daloth's death and Zayn's abduction. The burning of the pavilion. Cyrll offered, "I'll show you. Come."

Kalia was leaving. She blew Thayn a kiss. He watched his mother slip through the door.

She had endured so much. Surely, he could do the same.

*

Kalia returned home from the Center with a sack of purplefruit, pretending to have visited the marketplace. She agreed to share with her household nothing that she had learned about Thayn and Vok. Meetings with her son would take place in secret. Nobody else needed to know.

She passed the library and the school, smiling at anyone she knew. Thinking of Daloth, they looked at her with sympathetic eyes. Kalia slipped through the archway of her nexus and followed its crooked walkways home.

To her relief no neighbors waited to sit with her. Kalia felt as if she had been cheering them up instead of the other way around.

Eril, Neela and Zod were in school. Jiara and Zylla napped with the little ones. Dirak wove at his loom in an alcove.

Kalia retrieved Lo, her daughter by Daloth, from the nursery and returned to the main room. Weavings lay everywhere on the floor. She placed Lo on one of them and sat next to her.

Her mind wandered again to the Fallow Field. She thought about the statues of High Ministers that defined it. Perhaps, she imagined, Lo would be a great woman someday.

*

Cyrll, Thayn and Jad left the Center. Storm clouds edged the sky. They entered the Great Path, robed and hooded. Thayn collided with someone who stepped out of the shadow. "Oh."

"You?" Axl, the crazy man, glared at Thayn. He yelled after the retreating Woodswarder, "You don't belong here."

*

The Wooden Wall swung open in advance of the High Warden. Thayn and – lagging behind – Jad followed Cyrll through an understory of bushes and ferns to the High Camp. Thayn's eyes grew wide as they entered the pavilion. It was ravaged. Fallen gnarlwood had been replaced with tender cuttings. The remaining trunks were black, their branches ashen.

He turned, waiting for Jad.

Cyrll admitted, "None of us know how to care for him."

"I do. My father's the same way. He'll do as he's told, but – it'll take – "

The pavilion was checkered with light. Thayn looked up into the great, green vault of the Ring. It rippled in the wind.

* Chapter Nineteen *

After a moment Cyrll asked, " – time?"

Despite everything that happened, Thayn found comfort in a leafy sky.

Jad, at last, arrived. Thayn smiled sadly. He replied, "Yes, time."